TONY WILLIAMS's *All the Bananas I've Never
Eaten* won the Saboteur Award for best short story
collection. His poetry includes *The Corner of Arundel
Lane and Charles Street* and *The Midlands*. He lived in
Sheffield for more than a decade before moving to rural
Northumberland. He works in Newcastle-upon-Tyne.

TONY WILLIAMS

NUTCASE

SALT

LONDON

PUBLISHED BY SALT PUBLISHING 2017

2 4 6 8 10 9 7 5 3 1

First published in Great Britain in 2017 by
Salt Publishing Ltd
International House, 24 Holborn Viaduct, London EC1A 2BN United Kingdom

www.saltpublishing.com

Salt Publishing Limited Reg. No. 5293401

A CIP catalogue record for this book is available from the British Library

ISBN 978 1 78463 106 2 (Paperback edition)
ISBN 978 1 78463 107 9 (Electronic edition)

Typeset in Neacademia by Salt Publishing

Printed and bound in Great Britain by Clays Ltd, St Ives plc

Salt Publishing Limited is committed to responsible forest management.
This book is made from Forest Stewardship Council™ certified paper.

NUTCASE

MICK WILSON WAS a man of steel. He would work a shift without cracking a smile and then go home and eat his tea with Marie and the kid, saying nowt, and then go on to the Dog & Partridge and stand at the bar and sink six pints, saying nowt, and then go home to bed. Where sometimes, but not often, he would insist with Marie.

'You should use a johnny,' she said. 'We don't want another, at our age.'

Sometimes he'd had enough of Marie. All she was interested in was her fucking soaps. So he ignored her and carried on.

The kid, who was called Davey, was a waste of space. He wore hair gel. He missed school to go smoking weed up the railway line. He sneered when Mick asked him about coming to the works.

'Dead end that is. May as well cut out the middleman and get straight on the dole.'

This was back in the days when Thatcher was shagging the steel industry up the arse.

Mick said, try a cutlers shop then, or there was always labouring. But Davey signed up to college, which meant pootling off to a seminar three mornings a week and shagging that Becky and drinking cider in the afternoons. In the evenings, when Mick was sitting down to his tea and Davey was about to go off out with his mates, the two of them would have these terrible rows. Marie had to shut the living room door and turn up the telly.

It was worse if they happened to get in from the pub at the same time. They waved their arms and raved at each other, with their eyes rolling around their pissed faces. The swearwords spewed out of their mouths like sick. Then one day Mick completely lost it and gave Davey the old Wilson right hook. Except he lost his footing and missed, and put his fist through the frosted glass of the door.

All the time Marie was calling the ambulance, Davey was laughing and saying, 'You stupid fucking old cunt. It's a good job you fucking missed.'

The next week, Davey signed up to go and work on the rigs.

'It's good money,' he said to Marie. She was crying the whole time he was packing up his stuff, and Becky was there saying, 'We'll be able to afford our own place now. You and Mick'll have a bit of peace,' but Marie just kept crying. Mick was downstairs with a face like thunder, off work with his cut hand, and Marie was snivelling.

'I don't know what the problem is,' said Becky, who saw Davey as the perfect boy, pretty like Emilio Estevez but sensitive like Rob Lowe.

'Oh, just fucking leave it,' said Davey, and toted the holdall over his shoulder. Marie watched them down the street.

Becky was right: it was good money on the rigs, and it suited Davey fine, popping down every few weeks to shag her senseless and drink himself silly, then fuck off again on the train to Aberdeen where he didn't have to think about her except for a lovey-dovey five-minute phone call before he went to sleep. Of course, with all the shagging she got up the

4

duff, and it was good to miss all the throwing up too. But as it happened, he was on shore leave when the birth happened, so he could go in and see her the next day.

It was a boy. It looked like any other baby. They called it Ryan. 'Him,' said Becky, but Davey ignored her.

Because they'd sort of fallen out with Mick and Marie, and Davey was away most of the time on the rigs, Becky moved out of the flat and back in with her mum and dad in Leeds. When Davey came back, it wasn't the same any more: Becky's mum and dad were hanging around, in the way, and although he loved little Ryan there was only so much pushing prams round parks you could do. Having a baby also made it a lot harder to find time to jump in the sack. So sometimes he only called in for a night in Leeds and then pushed on to his mate Arshan's in Sheffy for some spliffs and cans.

'I'll just fucking kill myself, then shall I,' said Becky one time as he was getting up to go. 'You just want to come down here and screw me and then you fuck off again. And what about Ryan? Don't you care about him? He doesn't even know who you are. He just looks at you funny like you was a stranger and grabs on tighter.'

'And whose fault's that, then?' said Davey, even though he knew it was his.

And the funny thing was, she didn't kill herself, but a month or so later Becky died of hypovolemic shock from an undiagnosed ectopic pregnancy, and that was that. Out of the blue. The doctor kept saying it was very rare, but these things did happen. 'I bet they fucking do,' said her dad, 'only not to people who live in big houses out by Otley.' Davey threatened to sue the hospital, but of course that was just a lot of hot air.

Becky's mum was like a sad robot, keeping going and businesslike through her tears. She collared Davey. 'I think it's best if Ryan stays with us, don't you? You're not interested in the poor little bugger.'

Davey bristled up ready for a fight, but then he stopped and thought about it. Becky's little brother and sister were there playing with Ryan and he was giggling and hiccuping, and Davey thought, 'Christ yes, he's well shot of me,' so he said, 'Aye, alright.' And he got on the train back to Aberdeen with eight cans of Stella and told the poor sod next to him all about how he was a free man again, but wasn't it sad that his girlfriend had died, he loved her really, but heigh-ho never mind, about a hundred and twenty-seven times.

Somehow life on the rigs, which had all been a big lads' adventure when there was Becky to escape from, was a bit more depressing now that she was dead and he had a lot of time to think about her smile and the way she used to tickle his feet and so on. And he couldn't count down the days till he called in to see her on the way to Arshan's. There was just the rig – all that grey choppy sea heaving away day after day. He got a bit sick of it. And then it didn't matter anyway, because he'd failed one of the drugs tests they did periodically, and he got the sack. So he turned up at Arshan's with his old battered holdall and asked to kip on his sofa.

'Sure,' said Arshan, who figured he could do with another pair of hands when he went debt collecting.

It was good for a week or so, but then Arshan started to look pissed off when he came down in the morning to see Davey stretched out in front of the telly stinking of overnight farts. So Davey put his name down for a council flat, signed on, and got himself some cash-in-hand labouring. He sold a bit of Arshan's weed for him, on the side. It was good money, all that, when you added it up.

When Marie called to say Mick had died, heart attack, he got on a bus and went to the funeral. He even took her flowers. And after that he called in every Sunday for a gravy dinner.

2

ONE TIME DAVEY popped round to Arshan's to pick up a bag of skunk and there was this girl there, feet propped up on the arm of the sofa, doing her nails.

'Hello,' said Davey. 'You're alright.'

She looked him up and down and raised an eyebrow disdainfully, but you could tell she was impressed.

'She's alright,' he said to Arshan, as they were setting up the scales on the kitchen table.

'Who is?'

'Her.' Davey gestured next door. 'Your new bird.'

'Oh, Jasmine? It's not like that. She's, like, a second cousin or something. She's staying for a while. Why? You like her?'

Davey did. So he took Jasmine out clubbing a few times, and they started to wake up in bed together the next morning with stinking heads and big healthy appetites like you get after a night of exercise. After a while she moved into his flat, and not long after that the exercise had its effect: they started sprogging off and the council moved them into a pebble-dashed semi.

'Where are you from?' Marie asked Jasmine when they met. 'I mean originally.'

But Jasmine said, 'Bolton,' and poured herself another spritzer.

Marie said, 'Should you be drinking that?' and Jasmine said, 'Nope.'

When Davey got back from the lav, they were sat in silence – Marie fuming, Jasmine cool as you like.

'She's common as, that one,' said Marie, next time Davey came round on his tod. 'You know they wipe their arse with their hands, don't you?'

'So do you, you daft cow,' said Davey.

'That's not what I mean and you know it. I use toilet paper.'

'So the only difference between you and her is a sheet of bogroll?'

'Two sheets,' said Marie in an icy whisper. 'I fold it over.'

That was the end of the gravy dinners, but Davey and Jasmine were having more fun at home of a Sunday, listening to tunes and smoking some of that good weed of Arshan's. Davey was a bit worried at first in case some other cousins who were a bit less chilled out than Arshan might come round and string him up by his balls, but Jasmine just laughed and said it wasn't that sort of family. So they settled down and got quite well-known on the estate, walking the dog and selling weed, Davey knocking lads' heads together if they got too rowdy, having these barbecues and letting the whole street come along.

In Davey's head, it was like *The Godfather*. But instead of fruit stalls and big black sedans and pizza restaurants, it was boarded-up pubs and curry houses that did pizzas and burgers as well, deadlocks and barbed wire, flytipping and rats and burnt-out cars turning up in the woods. Then the local nature types would come and do a litter pick, with a special yellow tub for 'sharps', which meant the smackheads' needles. Davey would let the dog chase them back to their branded Puntos and give them the rods while they glared out at him, calling the police on their mobile phones.

It was the sort of area where social workers said, 'She'll do *what* for a choc ice?'

And because Davey wasn't a smackhead and Jasmine had been nearly twenty-two when they met, he thought of himself as Mr Responsible.

'Mr Responsible for this country going to the dogs,' said old Nev, who read the *Express* and had a heart condition. He thought people like Jasmine should be sent back to Pakistan or wherever, but he always had a good look at her arse when he stood behind her in Costcutter.

3

D AVEY AND JASMINE had four kids: Kayla, Amy, Nick, and Aidan.

Kayla was the oldest and trained as a beautician, then married this mad bugger called Steven Cox and spent her whole life visiting him in Belmarsh. Kayla could have done something with her life – you could imagine her as a paramedic, or something, if things had turned out differently. Amy was the total opposite, so knackered by booze and smack at nineteen that Davey and Jasmine were already picking out tunes for the crematorium, but then she met this completely straight car salesman called Martin and went off to live in a Barratt home far away from anyone she could score off. Martin pampered her like a princess and kept the door locked, and it was all a bit creepy like he wanted her to rely on him so he could control her, but at least she was clean most of the time.

Nick was quiet and kept his head down, took up boxing at thirteen and went to technical college after he left school. Everyone liked him, though his little brother Aidan said he was as boring as rugby league. Nick had a face that made people feel like they could trust him. He appeared on the last series of *Blind Date*, but he wasn't picked. It was such a shame.

Aidan was something else. Even as a little kid he was a mouthy bugger – right sarky, and hard with it. Swearing at teachers, setting fire to litter bins, smashing windows.

Swearing at the police who picked him up and took him to school, then waiting till they'd gone and walking out again. That time he slapped the deputy head. Trouble, basically. Davey didn't take to him ('He's a little shit'), but he was Jasmine's favourite, and she let him get away with murder.

When he was nine, Davey came in and told Aidan to clean his trainers, but instead Aidan smeared them in dog shit and chucked them up on the roof of the bus stop.

'You little bastard,' said Davey, but Jasmine said it was just a prank and boys would be boys.

Another time, Davey asked Aidan to get him a can of Stella from the fridge and a spliff that he had ready rolled on the worktop. Aiden went, but after a while he didn't come back so Davey went to look for him. He found him sitting up a tree in the park, drinking the beer and smoking the spliff. Davey started effing and blinding, as you would, till Aidan chucked the nearly full can at his head and half brained him. So Davey's effing and blinding some more and shaking the tree, and Aidan's laughing his head off and shouting, 'Fuck off grandad!' at the top of his voice.

All the local kids were standing round pissing themselves, and Davey was totally humiliated. When Aidan eventually came home, Davey gave him a bit of a whack, but Jasmine kept an eye on things to save him from a proper beating.

There was a pervert who used to hang about the wilder end of the park where it led on to the allotments and the back of the railway line. He used to hide in the bushes and flash at the kids who took a short cut through the fence to get to the estate. The kids never said anything to grown-ups about him

12

because it didn't occur to them. The flasher was just one of those dangers you had to cope with on your way home from school, like dog shit and barbed wire and older kids kicking you in the face.

He would step forward with a funny grin on his face and open his coat, and there would be this big red stiffy, all knobbly bits and wrinkles like a turkey's neck. Usually the kids would just look at it and stop talking and go white, and keep walking till they were past.

As far as they knew he had never dragged anyone into the bushes and strangled them, but that was like obviously what he had in the back of his mind, and the kids sort of knew that when he stepped out in front of them and they saw his thing and felt sick.

Then one day Aidan was walking home with a few others. He had an empty Coke can that he had ripped open into a metal ribbon, for no particular reason, and he was swinging it round like a chain as he walked. The flasher stepped out from the bushes and opened his coat, and there was this horrible shining cock all close up in front of their faces.

They all stopped and stood there, and then Aidan stepped forward and swung the torn-open Coke can at the pervert's cock. Straight away a load of blood spurted from the cock where the metal had cut it, down at the base towards the loose skin of his nutsack. Aidan jumped back out of the way of the spurting blood, and then they all stood and laughed at the flasher while he clamped his hands over his knob and tried to stop the blood coming out. But it wouldn't stop coming. It was running all over his hands and down his legs, and his stiffy melted away in no time. Then the flasher pulled his coat back round him and ran off across the park, whispering, 'You fucking little bastard,' but not daring to shout in case it made the dog walkers turn round and look.

Aidan was a hero at primary school for like a week after that. Until the incident with the Mr Freezes in the girls' bogs.

4

BY THIS TIME, Davey and Jasmine had had another baby, a boy called Jay, and even though he had been an accident, Davey worshipped the ground he walked on. Now that Davey had calmed down a bit and wasn't so bothered about getting completely off it all the time, it was like he was going to try to be a proper dad to Jay, and the others and in particular Aidan could fuck off out of it. Davey would buy these spenny glass jars of food for the baby, but Aidan was lucky if he got chips and scraps.

'That's charming, that is,' said Aidan. 'When you have a midlife crisis it's your bird you're supposed to trade in for a younger model, not your kids.'

But Davey had found out about Aidan nicking his fags, and he gave him a couple of hard cuffs to the lip.

When Aidan was twelve, Davey and Jasmine took little Jay away for a night or two at Filey. Davey said to Aidan, 'Don't burn the place down, will you,' and gave him thirty quid. He told him to make sure he walked the dog, and said that if he didn't and she shat everywhere, Aidan would be the one who had to clear it up.

The dog was a four-year-old staffie called Meg. She was alright with the family, but with strangers and other dogs she was like Gnasher. All yapping and straining and bared teeth and that. It gave Aidan a headache.

The first night he took her up to the park and let her run

around a bit. She nearly caught a duck, and then had a go at this bloke's pug. The bloke picked up the pug and was trying to bollock Aidan, but he still had Meg jumping up at him trying to get the pug, and he was having to sort of kick her away without getting bitten.

'Sorry,' said Aidan, trying to grab her collar to pull her away. The bloke was telling him off like an angry science teacher. Once Aidan had Meg on the lead he just walked off. On the way home he kept shouting at her, because although the bloke had been a dick about it, Aidan knew that it was Meg's fault or more to the point Davey's for not training her properly.

In the morning he took her out again, the other way this time, down to the woods at the other end of the estate. She ran off again, and this time when he caught up with her she had this cat by the back leg, ragging it about, trying to kill it. Aidan tried to get her jaws apart with his hands and ended up with cuts from her teeth and the cat's claws. He picked up a big branch that was lying about and started laying into her with it. He had to hit the dog a lot of times before she'd let go of the cat, and then when he was dragging her home she was walking funny, sort of limping with her whole body.

When Davey got home and saw her he went apeshit. She had basically just laid in her bed the whole time since Aidan got her back. Davey got Jasmine to take her down the vet's, and it turned out she had a broken leg and broken ribs and some internal injuries and had to be put down, and Jasmine and Davey narrowly avoided getting prosecuted for animal cruelty.

'It weren't my fault,' said Aidan. 'She was killing this cat.'

This time Jasmine didn't stop Davey giving him a proper

leathering. It was the first and last time that happened. After that, Aidan got too big for Davey to risk it. And after that the two of them permanently fell out, even though they lived in the same house, ignoring each other, staying out of each other's way. All the rest of his life Aidan was missing one of his bottom front teeth because of the leathering he got for killing Meg the dog.

He got up to all sorts of other stuff, too. The usual: nicking stuff, getting pissed, skiving school. He burned a lad's neck with a heated-up Zippo and tripped Ian Haynes in the Gala Bingo car park, and broke his leg. He paid Kelly Stone a quid to let him draw lipstick specs on her tits and a big gob where her belly button was, and then to pull her pants down to make a beard. It turned out Kelly Stone didn't have much hair yet so it was like a wispy goatee. After that it seemed like he should do something else, so he threw a breeze block through the window of the oriental supermarket and then asked her to go down on him. But Kelly Stone ran away and didn't seem to like him after that.

There was the time he opened all the cages in the pet shop, and the time he fired his air pistol at the tram from the roof of Jack Fultons Frozen Foods, and the paint he sprayed all over the gates of the meat paste factory. But he was usually smart enough not to get caught, and the day he killed his own dad's dog was the mentallest thing he did, and the thing he was best known for, growing up.

5

THERE WERE ALL sorts of young lads who used to hang about on the estate. Some of them were dicks, but some of them were alright.

Nick knew these brothers, Carl and Connor, who used to go with him to the boxing gym. But old Stu had had to stop taking the sessions because of the trouble with his prostate, so they ditched the gloves and started meeting up for bare knuckle fights in the service yard behind the incinerator. It was just for fun. No money changed hands, and they had a rule that you couldn't go for the other person's face. After a couple of weeks they were all walking around really gingerly as if they had sunburn, with big bruises like mildew under their tops. But their faces were clean so their bosses and mums and social workers couldn't bend their ears about it.

One Saturday morning when Aidan was about thirteen, he went with Nick to see if they could get this motorbike out of the canal. Some kid had nicked it the night before, ridden it up and down the Parkway and then chucked it in. One handlebar and mirror were visible above the surface of the water. Nick had this idea they could get it out and clean it up and sell it.

'It'll be knackered,' said Aidan, but he went along anyway because it was a sunny day and there was fuck-all else to do.

There was already a crowd there when they arrived – Carl and Connor and one or two others, and a few little shrimps who were always hanging around. Connor had told one of the shrimps to wade out to the bike, and now he was sat on the bodywork with the canal up to his belly, enjoying the attention.

'Take the other end of this,' Connor was saying, and trying to fling out one end of a length of blue nylon rope so he could catch it.

'Get off it and stand it up,' someone else was shouting.

The others were saying, 'Watch out for sharks,' and, 'Chuck summat at him.' And, 'Knock the little fucker off.'

And the little shrimp was giving them all the rods and grinning.

'This is a waste of time,' said Aidan, and sat down on the wall and smoked a Lambert & Butler.

After a while someone brained the shrimp with a lump of loose concrete they'd found on the towpath, and he fell in the canal and climbed out.

'You fucking bastards,' he kept saying. 'I'm going to get my dad.'

They jeered, but the next thing a plod car pulled up on the bridge above them, and though they hadn't done anything against the law they had enough sense to run. The next thing, they ended up in the service yard, which was sort of a safe haven for them, and Carl and Connor started setting up one of their fights.

Aidan got matched up against this dude called Foxy, who was nearly seventeen, and Nick said he was a half-cousin or something. He was walking round Aidan in a circle giving him these little jabs to the chest. Aidan hadn't been to one of the fights before, and although he'd been told about the no faces rule, he hadn't really been paying attention. So after Foxy had danced round him a couple of times, giving him these tap-taps on the chest, Aidan lamped him.

It wasn't a proper hit – it didn't catch him right. But it bloodied Foxy's nose and he came right back at Aidan and caught him under the ear and stamped at his leg, and the next thing they were fully going at it, swinging each other round by the shirt and kicking the shit out of each other. Carl and Connor and Nick managed to pull them apart. Everyone was laughing and swearing, Aidan was spitting blood on to the floor, and Foxy was looking at where his sleeve had got torn. Nick was still holding Aidan's arms but he said, 'Alright, I'm not a fucking dog, you can let me off the lead now,' and Connor was laughing and saying, 'Calm down, twats,' and they did.

On the way home Aidan said to Nick, 'I could have had him, easy.'

'Yeah,' said Nick, like he wasn't impressed.

But Carl said, 'He's not bad at fighting, your brother,' to Nick, and even though he said it as if Aidan wasn't there, you could tell it was meant to be a compliment.

6

A YEAR OR so after that, Arshan came to stay with Davey and Jasmine while his own house was being fumigated for bed bugs. He was worth a bob or two now – he ran his uncle's restaurant and owned a couple of minicabs that operated out of a first-floor flat on Sharrowvale Road. Plus he was still shifting healthy amounts of weed. They sat out the back grilling Savers chicken breasts and drinking Red Stripe.

'How are the boys getting on, then?' asked Arshan, wiping his can across his brow. It was dead hot. Jasmine was sitting there in just her bra.

'Nick's doing alright. He'll be done with his apprenticeship next year, and then he'll be on good money.'

'And Aidan?'

Davey made a face and guffed. 'He doesn't listen to a word I say. Whatever he ends up doing, it'll be what Aidan wants. He won't be told.'

'He's a big lad.'

'Aye, and he's got a big mouth, too. It'll get him into trouble. I try not to let it get to me but I know we're going to have an almighty bust-up one day.'

After the chicken they carved up a mint Viennetta. Arshan said, 'A few of us are going to Amsterdam next weekend. It'll be carnage. We could take him along, get him out of your hair for a few days?'

'Awesome,' said Davey, and it was all arranged.

'No whores or Class As,' said Jasmine, fiddling with her straps.

There was a group of twelve of them. 'Like the fucking apostles,' said Arshan, but they all gave him blank looks. They got a National Express to Newcastle then piled on to the ferry. Arshan had said to bring some cans so they didn't have to pay the ferry prices. Aidan had a bag of Carlings from Londis, a couple of packets of ready salted and a steak bake.

They sat in the lounge area and drank for a bit, then headed off on deck, some to chuck up and the others to laugh at them and throw sandwiches for the birds. Aidan came inside again and played for a while on an old Virtua Cop 3 console, trying to impress these posh girls from Harrogate, but then their teacher turned up. So he went back to the seats where his stuff was, but all his cans had gone. There was just a few crisps trodden into the carpet.

He steamed round the lounge and then out on deck, and found this mate of Arshan's, Shaun something, finishing a mouthful of food over a Carling.

'Have you had my beer?' said Aidan.

'You what?' said Shaun something.

'You heard,' said Aidan, and caught him a smack round the side of the head.

This Shaun wasn't much older than Aidan, and he wasn't half the size. Before he'd got up Aidan had given him a few more in the head, and the last one sent his head back hard against a metal stairway. He gave him a few kicks in the ribs, and then heard voices coming so walked quickly off round the corner.

Back in the lounge they asked him if he'd seen Shaun.

'Yeah,' he said, jabbing his thumb over his shoulder. 'Some fucker's kicked his head in. It's them United fans.'

'Is it fuck,' said Arshan, looking into Aidan's face, which was kind of shining as if he was really high or pissed. But he only said, 'We'd better go and make sure he's alright, then.'

Some dude, a big steroid-popper who was Shaun's uncle or something, had steam coming out of his ears, but he couldn't get at Aidan there in full view of everyone. 'You've fucking had it, sunshine,' he said, drawing his finger across his throat.

Aidan blew him a kiss.

'Oh, for fuck's sake,' said Arshan.

Anyway, it didn't matter because the ferry CCTV had caught the whole thing, and when they got into IJmuiden the Dutch police were waiting. Aidan had to stay on the ferry to go back and face the music in Newcastle. Jasmine had to come up on the train and pay fifty quid police bail.

'Your dad's off his nut,' she said. 'You can't come home or he'll wring your neck. And anyway Shaun's uncles'll kill you if they find you on the estate.'

They decided that Aidan should stay up in Newcastle for the time being. There was a bloke called Ross who ran an iffy business delivering white goods and furniture, who Jasmine knew from way back.

'Is he an ex?' said Aidan.

'He wishes.'

7

THEY MET ROSS in the car park of a pub in Byker. He said he'd heard Aidan was a real ball-ache, but he looked strong so he'd take him. 'There's a spare room at my flat. No shagging my daughter. Do as I say and we'll be fine.'

'How old's your daughter?' asked Aidan, and Jasmine clipped him round the ear.

'Shut up,' she said. 'For all you know she's your half-sister.'

They both looked at her.

She counted out two hundred quid in twenties and gave it to him. 'Don't take any shit from anyone,' she said, 'but don't give none either. And use a rubber.'

Aidan grinned. Then they all got in the front of Ross's Transit, dropped her at the Metro station and drove up the dual carriageway to the depot.

'Fit, your mum,' said Ross.

Aidan put his feet up on the dashboard and said nothing.

The depot turned out to be a grotty warehouse unit where some Somali lads were hefting boxes about on sack barrows and arguing with each other in Somalian.

'What are they saying?' said Aidan.

'Who gives a fuck?' said Ross, and bogged off again in his van.

Whether they were illegals wasn't clear, but it was obviously cash in hand. Every few minutes a van would arrive back, and they'd stack it up quick with stuff, and then the driver and his mate would hop in and speed off to deliver it. Aidan sat on his arse and watched them, drinking a banana Frijj. A couple of times they asked him to help, but he just laughed at them. 'Work harder!' he said. 'Lazy bastards!'

After Ross had got back, the Somalians had a word with him, and he came and had a word with Aidan.

'It's pissing them off a bit, you sat about not helping. They say you're looking for a hiding.'

'That'd liven things up. I reckon I could take out three of them before they had me.'

Ross shook his head. 'You haven't got a clue, have you? Just do some fucking work. I've had word HMRC might come down here later, and we need to get all this crap shifted before they do.'

So Aidan leapt up and started grappling boxes around. They were all amazed at what he could do, for a kid. He lifted washing machines on his tod, one after another, and had to be stopped in the end when the transit he was loading was right down on its axles. The Somalis were more friendly then, offering him fags, and when the gear was all gone and they were about to make themselves scarce, in case HMRC did show up (although this was probably a lie Ross made up to make them work quicker), they gave Aidan a pouch of khat.

'You did OK,' said Ross on the way home. 'Sometimes you just have to keep your head down. They're good lads. You've got a face for attracting trouble - you don't need to go looking for it.'

Yeah, yeah - he sounded like Davey. Aidan looked out of

the window at the kebab shops and bookies and the girls in short skirts walking down the pavement.

'I bet you wank about my mum, don't you?' he said.

'Sometimes,' said Ross.

8

L IFE WITH ROSS was alright. Some days Aidan would go to work with him, picking stuff up, lugging it around, in return for his board and a bit of cash. Some days he wouldn't bother, but would just lie about in the morning watching daytime telly. Ross's daughter Sally would walk through wrapped in towels from the shower and they would be rude to each other in that spiky flirting way, but Aidan wasn't quite sure how to take things further. She was like nineteen or something, and he didn't want to come across as a stupid kid. After she'd gone to college he might toss himself off, and then get dressed and have a wander up through the estate.

There was a pub with a flat roof called The Coal Barge, and Aidan took to hanging about the beer garden in the afternoons with a man called Eddie. Eddie was a doler with smudged old tattoos on his hands, and a bit creepy. What was he doing hanging around with a young lad? But Aidan figured he could kick the shit out of him no probs, so it was safe to let him buy him beer. Eddie went on about all sorts of shit – Tories, pervs, Mackems, MPs, Shearer and coke. He said he'd been invalided out of the Royal Regiment of Fusiliers, but it seemed more likely he was just a lying twat.

He'd say, 'Scargill had it right. A line of coppers and a line of us, going at it. Class war. That's what it's all about.'

'Who's Scargill?' said Aidan, and Eddie cracked a wry face and pulled on his rollie.

Below the pub was a little park, and one day Aidan saw Sally come in and sit down on a bench and sit there crying.

'What's up with her,' said Eddie. 'I'd cheer her up.'

'Shut up you knobend,' said Aidan. He watched her for a while, and when she left he followed her – down to the river and along to the Quayside, up to the Monument, round and about, window-shopping. In the end she went down into the Metro system, and he walked home.

When he got back, she was in the kitchen cooking Super Noodles.

'Good day at college?'

'Not bad,' she said, without turning round.

'Bollocks. I saw you bawling your eyes out in the park. What's going on?'

And while the Super Noodles were catching on the hob she started bawling her eyes out again, saying, 'You can't tell me Dad,' till Aidan thought she was just a wet skiver who didn't want to get caught. But then she told him that one of her tutors had been coming on to her – getting her to come to these one-to-one meetings, saying how sexy she was, touching her arse and so on. Then one day he felt her tit and pushed her up against the filing cabinet in his office. It took a long time to tell all this because she was proper sobbing now. 'And he – *uhh! uhh!* – locked the door and – *uhh! uhh-hee!* – opened his flies up and *uhh-hee-hee! uhh!* – m-made us hold it. *And,*' she said, whispering now, '*he come in me hand.*'

Aidan was doing his best to do the comforting thing, but now he got up and started walking round and round the flat. 'I'll kill the bastard,' he kept saying, 'I'll kill the bastard.'

'No! You can't! No, please. He'll get us chucked off me course. He'll fail me. Don't go down there. *Please.*'

He pulled down the lampshade and kicked it to bits, then sat down and said, 'We've got to tell your dad, then,' and when Ross came back from the warehouse, they did.

He did the pacing the flat and breaking some of the fittings thing too, and then gave Sally a big cuddle, doing that comforting thing a sight better than Aidan had. 'There's always the law,' he said, but she said, 'No, Dad, no,' to that too, and you could see to look at her how ashamed and desperate she was already with only the two of them knowing.

'Maybe this'll be the end of it,' said Ross. 'Now he's – had his fun – if you go back to class and ignore him and don't go to any meetings if he asks.'

But apparently this guy had said he was 'sick of her being a tease', and next time they were going to 'do things properly', and Sally was adamant that if she didn't go then he'd fail her and she'd get chucked off her course.

'It doesn't work like that,' said Ross. 'Does it?'

'Dunno,' said Aidan, who had a kind of faraway look in his eyes. 'I want to see this bloke.' He said he wanted to see the lie of the land, and told Sally to go in to class as normal the next day and point out the tutor to him.

'Oh God, you'll put him in hospital,' she said, but Aidan promised her he wouldn't.

The next morning he got up and drank a mug of tea and then a half-pint of vodka with some orange in it, and smoked fags on the balcony till Sally was ready to go. On the way out he picked up a pair of marigolds from under the kitchen sink.

In the big open area the college people called the atrium Sally stood back with Aidan, and pointed out the tutor, Peter, as everyone was filing into the seminar room. Aidan sat on a sofa and looked at the girls in a course prospectus for an hour, and when the class came out he kept out of sight of Sally but followed this Peter up the stairs and along the corridor to his office. He put the marigolds on and then knocked on the door, opened it, went in and shut it again.

'Can I help you?' said Peter, who was perched on his desk leafing through some papers.

'It's about my friend Sally.'

Peter's face hardens, but before he has a chance to speak Aidan's punched him, hard, in the throat. He sprawls backwards over the desk with his eyes rolling, choking for breath. Next thing Aidan has him by the collar and he's saying, 'Make a noise and I'll kill you,' and Peter doesn't make a peep. Aidan's eyes wander vaguely over the desk, and then he spies a pair of scissors and picks them up. 'Trousers down,' he says, and when Peter hesitates he holds the scissors up close to his face.

Peter's still bent backwards over his attendance registers and computer keyboard. He's undone his flies and Aidan's pulled his trousers and boxers down around his ankles. He grabs Peter's dick by the foreskin and pulls it hard, stretching it out like a rubber band. Peter gasps in pain and horror, but before he has a chance to do anything Aidan takes the scissors in his other hand and in one fast slice cuts through it so that the end of Peter's foreskin is left in his hand and the rest of his dick springs back, spraying blood all over his thighs and shirt tails. There's a lot of blood, straight away, lots of it covering Peter's legs and desk and splashing on to Aidan too. Peter still can't speak or even breath with the shock but he's going to get very noisy very soon.

'Get the message?' says Aidan, drops the scissors on the floor and walks quickly out of the office and down the stairs. By the time he reaches the atrium he's running, and

Peter's screams are starting to echo in the building behind him.

Back at the flat Aidan handed Ross an empty Skittles packet.

'What the fuck is that?' said Ross, looking inside.

When Aidan told him he went ape, and then he started to see the funny side, and then he started to go ape again. It was a lot to take in. 'Fuck,' he said. 'You fucking nutcase.'

Sally was sitting there wide-eyed. 'I'm off me course for sure,' she said. 'I'll go to prison.'

'You won't,' said Ross. 'He's out of here.' He handed Aidan the Skittles packet. 'Don't let a drop of that touch the flat. Get your things together and go. They won't be able to touch you then, Sal.'

Aidan laughed. 'Relax. I wore gloves, man. Anyway, you worry too much. What's he going to say? "This kid cut the end of my cock off cos I've been having it off with the students?"'

He packed his bag and Ross gave him fifty notes and said, 'Thanks.'

'Yeah, thanks,' said Sally, blushing, by the door.

It turned out that Aidan was right. No one ever asked Sally about what had happened, and there was never any sign of the police. Apparently an ambulance had turned up and taken Peter away, and he was off sick for the rest of the semester, and then again the next. Sally passed her course.

9

AIDAN WENT AND stayed with creepy Eddie on the other side of the estate, and put up with all his endless pornos and Toon Army bollocks because he let him share his ketamine and didn't charge any rent. He still did the odd day for Ross here and there, and life was pretty good. His sentence for beating Shaun up on the ferry was just a fine, and because he had only been fourteen at the time, it was Davey who had to pay.

The way Eddie was plying him with drugs and readies was a bit weird. Eddie said, 'You remind me of me son,' but his eyes kept darting from side to side.

'You never mentioned a son before,' said Aidan.

Apparently Eddie had a son and two daughters living in South Shields. He hadn't seen them since he nicked their mam's car to buy some brown, even though, since then, he had been clean for four years.

'Yeah,' said Aidan. There had been an empty bottle of methadone hanging about the place just the other week.

Then Eddie started giving Aidan chapter and verse on his car crash of a marriage and how his son and daughters hated him but only because his ex had poisoned them against him. 'Says I'm scum,' he said. 'She works at fucking Netto herself.'

'Yep,' said Aidan. For all the drugs sloshing around at Eddie's, life had been more fun living with Ross. He started hanging around with some other lads down at the kiddies' playground. There was an offie nearby where they didn't ask for ID. He got into a few scraps and won, and after that everyone started to be friendly. He spent his summer messing around getting pissed on the estate, and going back in the evenings to help Eddie get through his bags of pills and powders.

One night he came in and found Eddie monged out on the sofa surrounded by his own sick. He was grey-skinned and his heart was fluttering away. Aidan filled up the mop bucket with cold water and poured it over him, then did the same thing again twice more, and after that Eddie started to come round but he was shivering so much it was like a dog scratching itself with its back leg. So then Aidan got the duvets off his and Eddie's beds and put them over him. He whacked the heating up too, and after a while Eddie stopped shivering and started bawling like a baby.

'Fuck's sake,' Aidan said, and put the kettle on. When Eddie had come round and cleaned himself up, Aidan gave him the tail end of a spliff and the remains of a bottle of gin he had in his pocket, and told him to sort himself out.

After an hour or so Eddie was beginning to feel better, and he started going on about his kids again, saying he didn't want them growing up being ashamed of their dad.

Aidan said, 'That particular ship has already sailed, my friend.'

Eddie took exception to that and tried to land one on him, but Aidan dodged his head and put his fist into Eddie's stomach. Eddie was on his hands and knees retching and looking up with frightened eyes, but Aidan just put his jacket on and walked out.

He walked across the estate and got to Ross's place at quarter past two in the morning. There was a light on so he pressed the buzzer. Ross was eating cheese on toast and watching *Van Helsing*. He had had a bit to drink. It had been a few months since the thing with the tutor's foreskin, and there had been no come-back. So Ross said OK, Aidan could move back in, but the rule about not shagging Sally still applied.

10

THE FIRST MORNING back at the flat, Aidan was surprised to bump into some lad coming out of the bathroom in the morning. One of those big idiots with tattoos and a shaved, bodybuilder's chest.

'Oh, him,' said Ross when he asked. 'That's Darren, Sal's new bloke. He's a right twat, but what can you do?'

Darren wasn't pleased to have Aidan about the place, especially when he saw how well Aidan and Sally got on. He swaggered about the flat in his boxer shorts and made it clear that he thought Aidan was a piece of shit.

'You autistic?' he said. 'Don't forget your medication, elephant man.' And, 'When you going back to school?'

'Pull my finger,' said Aidan. He'd noticed that Sally didn't like it when Darren tried to pick on him, so he played the good kid and let it wash over him. He would sit quietly in front of *Casualty*, eating his Filet-o-Fish meal. He was eating a lot of fish, because he'd heard it was good for his brain.

During the day, when Darren was at work, Sally and Aidan would sometimes sit on the sofa and watch *Diagnosis Murder* together, and pretty soon Sally started leaning in to him so that Aidan could smell her hair, which smelled of shampoo, and they graduated to lying back in a cuddle, with Aidan playing with her hair and stroking it back behind her ear. Then one day they started snogging and then unzipped themselves and shagged each other, and after that it was a regular love nest from the moment Darren and Ross went out the door in the morning.

'I can't believe I'm doing this,' said Sally. 'You're only a baby. Are you sixteen yet? I could go to jail.'

Aidan did feel like a lucky sod. Sally was twenty and dead sophisticated.

She tried to be careful, but Aidan was always wanting to get busy without a condom on, and it was easy to get carried away. One day he came inside her, and she started fretting about getting up the duff.

'Would it be so bad?' asked Aidan, circling his finger round and round her belly button.

'Would it – course it fucking would. You've got no qualifications, you've got no job, I bet you haven't even got your cycling fucking proficiency.'

He was offended. 'I could do more days for your dad. We'd be alright.'

'Fuck!' She had her head in her hands. This wasn't how she'd wanted things to be. The upshot was that she made him go with her down to the sexual health clinic to hold her hand while she got a morning-after pill. He got a pasty from Greggs on the way.

Back at the flat, Sally went to bed. Aidan watched *The Bourne Conspiracy* on DVD, and then took her in some tea and toast. They cuddled up and talked for a bit, and then Aidan started to get ideas, but Sally said her stomach felt a bit gippy and her tits were sore, so he left her to sleep and walked in to the city centre, bored.

He ended up bumping into a lad he knew and went to drink cans up Jesmond Dene. When they were pissed up, Sally sent a text saying Darren was back from work, so Aidan stayed out and ended up kipping on his mate's sofa out in Fenham.

The next day he walked back to the flat. He could hear raised voices as he got near the door, and as soon as he got in, Darren was in his face.

'What's gone on here, you little spack?'

It was obvious he didn't know about Aidan and Sally, but something was up. The leaflet that came with the morning-after pill was lying screwed up on the coffee table. 'You went with her, did you? Fucking egging her on to kill my kid.'

'Don't be a bellend,' said Aidan. Sally's bedroom door was open but he couldn't see her.

'Don't be a fucking bellend! My mate fucking saw you. "Your bird and some kid," he says, "Quite a big lad." Anyway I know it was you cause she fucking said so.' He jabbed his thumb towards the bedroom.

'Oh aye, smack it out of her did you?' Aidan was standing quite still, watching Darren as he stormed round the place.

'I dint fucking have to. She telt us straight up.'

'You fucking liar,' Sally's voice came from the bedroom.

Aidan feinted to send a right hook at Darren, who flinched. Aidan laughed. Then Ross came in the front door and saw them squaring up to each other, and said , 'Not in my house, you twats.' And he called through the bedroom door, 'What they fighting about, Sal?'

'Darren hit me.'

'Right. In that case,' he nodded to Aidan, 'carry on.'

So Aidan gave Darren a kicking. Even though Darren was ten years older and six inches taller, Aidan had him on the floor in three seconds: a right-left-right to the side of the head, a knee in the bollocks and then in the face, and then he was stamping on Darren's hands till Ross hauled him off in a bear hug.

Darren was juddering on the floor, trying to scream, with blood coming out of his nose and mouth and his left thumb hanging down at a bad angle.

'Fuck's sake,' said Sally, coming out of the bedroom in her dressing gown. Her face was all puffy. There was blood on the carpet and on the corner of the sofa. 'That's on HP that is, you can't send that back now.'

Darren was calming down and starting to get up on to all fours, or rather all threes since he was holding his knackered hand up under his chest. He'd stopped bellowing now, and they stood and watched him stagger up to his feet and walk out of the flat, then listened through the open door as he limped his way down the stairs.

Ross put the kettle on. 'You've been at it, you two, then?' he said, and Aidan and Sally had the good grace to look ashamed.

11

S OON IT WAS all over the estate that Darren had given
Sally a tap and then got given a leathering himself by the
kid who was staying in Ross's spare room. Darren liked to
give out that he was the big man, so it was pretty funny that a
kid had beaten him up. People sat in The Coal Barge and said
that Aidan must be a mad little bastard to do that. Somehow,
word had started to get out about what he had done to Sally's
tutor too. So he was kind of a hero. But the general consensus
was that he wouldn't last five minutes: either he would get
shot by a police marksman, or someone would slip a shank in
his intestines the first time he was on remand.

Darren's cousin, a lad called Stephen Finlay, started mouthing off in the Barge about how Aidan was going to get what
was coming to him. He sat at the bar drinking triple Bell's
telling Scot the barman how Aidan was going to cop a real
pasting. Scot was saving up so that he could give Claire, his
fiancée, the wedding she deserved. Claire had once done a
manicure for Michael Flatley. That was the level she was
working at. Scott was doing a degree in textiles part-time, but
he didn't tell people like Stephen Finlay that. The next time
Aidan came in, Scot told him what Stephen had been saying,
and Aidan bought him a pint to say thanks. After that Aidan
stopped walking around with his headphones in, so that no
one could jump him from behind.

One Saturday morning Aidan and Ross were wandering

down to Lidl to get some meat, beer and charcoal, because it looked like being another hot one. When they went past the Coral a man rushed out and tried to clout Aidan round the back of the head. Aidan had been thinking about which type of Haribo to buy, Starmix or Sourmix, and took a second to react, but Ross was walking a pace behind him and pushed Aidan out of the way so that the man's punch landed on him instead.

Ross fell headlong into the gutter and a bus going by had to brake hard to avoid popping his skull like a grape. He grovelled there for a moment and because he seemed to have come sprawling out of the betting shop, everyone assumed he was just another disgraceful drunk.

Meanwhile Aidan had turned round and recognised that the man was Stephen Finlay. He grabbed him by the sleeve, yanked him forward and headbutted him. Then, once Finlay was on his back, he stamped on his arm a few times and broke it in two places.

All the people in the cars that had stopped when the bus braked were watching, and shoppers were standing around not wanting to go past while the fight was happening in case they caught a stray punch. Aidan helped Ross get up and they jogged off down the alley by the chip shop in case some bugger had called the plod.

By lunchtime everyone was talking about it in The Coal Barge, saying that this time Aidan really was a dead man. The trouble was that Stephen Finlay's dad Michael Finlay, who Aidan hadn't even known existed, was just about to be let out of prison, and he had basically been the king of the estate four or five years ago, when he was last around. Aidan would probably end up in a bloody heap on the hard shoulder of the central motorway. Everyone said it was a shame, but that was what happened when boys started acting up like men.

The truth was that Michael Finlay was more of a fat middle-aged thug than an actual gangster. He swaggered around in a suit from Top Man and had to watch his blood sugar. The day he got out, him and Stephen got legless in the pub and went on about how they were going to chuck this kid off the Tyne Bridge. But when Michael lurched off for a piss he seemed to be gone for a long time. They found him picking his teeth out of the urinal, with his hair and the back of his Top Man jacket all soaked in piss. Scot the barman called him an ambulance and swore blind he hadn't seen anyone coming or going through the fire exit.

The next day Michael and Stephen turned up at Ross's place, but Ross met him in the stairwell with a bunch of his Somalian lads, all holding bits of two-by-four and adjustable spanners. 'He's not here,' he said. 'I chucked him out when I heard what he did.' Which was a total lie of course. Aidan was pacing about the flat, with Sally barring the door telling him if he went out there he'd get killed. But the Finlays didn't like the look of all those Somalians who had nothing to lose and had probably seen a fuck sight worse in that civil war of theirs. So Stephen shouted the odds for a bit and Michael made some low rumbling threats, and then they went away.

Ross said enough was enough, and anyway it was time Sally found a man her own age with a job and prospects. To be quite honest Aidan was a nice lad but it was draining having him around. So Aidan promised he would be gone by the end of the week.

The next thing was, someone superglued a dead cat to the windscreen of Michael Finlay's Nissan. No one knew if the cat died before or after Aidan got his hands on it. Karen Finlay, Michael's wife, found it and screamed. Her hands shook so much that day that she had to cancel all her appointments at the salon.

This time Ross didn't know the Finlays would be coming, so he and his lads were out delivering knocked-off fridges all over Tyneside. Sally was in the flat on her own and she shat herself as she listened to them smashing the bottom door open and then coming up and kicking in the door of the flat. They didn't touch her but they trashed the flat, chucking the plates out of the cupboards, upsetting the sofa and so on. Michael Finlay was a touch out of breath after coming up three flights of stairs, so most of the damage was cosmetic, but it shit Sally up something proper, and as soon as they had gone she rang Ross and gave him the SP.

Ross was livid. He rang Aidan and told him he better not turn up at the flat again. He thought the other day had been an end of it, but now this business with the cat meant it was all kicking off again. Ross said, if he ever saw Aidan again he would personally march him across the estate and hand him over to the Finlays.

Ross also gave Jasmine a call and told him what a mess her precious son was in. So Jasmine cooed in Davey's ear and he called Ryan, Aidan's half-brother who was still living in Leeds and working in IT sales, and asked him to go and fetch him before he got himself killed. So that afternoon Ryan bombed up the A1 and picked up Aidan from the Metrocentre.

'Nice to meet you,' he said. 'I've heard you're a right little fucker.'

They went back to Leeds and Aidan stayed for a week or two. They drank a lot of lager, getting to know each other, nattering on about what a bad dad Davey was. Then one Sunday when he had a girl coming round, Ryan put Aidan on a train back to Sheffy.

12

A IDAN HAD BEEN gone just over a year, but nothing much had changed. Davey and Jasmine were still living in the same house on the same estate. Arshan had died of cancer of the oesophagus. His son took over the taxi firm but Davey moved up the chain and started supplying weed to the estate. He got it off Karamat Kizil, who drove around in a 4×4 Nissan with blacked-out windows.

'Arshan was a good man, very steady,' he said. 'I'm sure you will be too.'

'Yep,' said Davey.

There was this kid called Joe who had grown up down the road and had got to know Davey and Jasmine pretty well. He always came to their barbecues and if Davey ever needed to get something delivered quickly, Joe would nip round on his bike and take it for him. Now he was nearly eighteen, and thinking of going into the army. Davey thought this was a mug's game, but Jasmine told Joe over the buns and salad that it would be good for him. 'Otherwise,' she said, 'you'll end up inside half your life.' Meanwhile it was summer and Joe was enjoying himself going to parties, shagging around, and picking up odd bits of scrap metal to sell to Davey's mate Dwayne.

That was the same summer that Shelley Turner and Mark Crabbe went a bit mental after Shelley's dad died of carbon monoxide poisoning. They went around drinking white cider and pulling knives on people, and everyone said it was Shelley who was the evil one and Mark was just going along with it because he was shagging her or a bit thick or scared of her, and probably all three. But Shelley had done Sociology A-level and said that was misogyny plain and simple, and when a man was hard everyone wanted to be his friend, but if a fit young woman was they said she was a sicko. Which was all very well but years later when it was in the national press about stabbing that horse and how she had kept an Armenian slave in the cellar of a house on Spital Hill , everyone including the Home Office psychologist concluded that she was a sicko after all.

Late in the summer Joe found out about a chained-up yard out by the allotments where there was a lot of old machinery and scrap. The business had gone bust and there was no one up there keeping watch, so he cut a way through the fence and started taking out the metal and selling it to Dwayne.

Mark Crabbe got to hear of this over a spliff with Joe's blabbermouth sister Sue, and the next night when Joe went up, he found Mark and Shelley there loading an industrial lathe on to the back of a pick-up. He said it was his stuff because he had found it and when they squared up to him he picked up a screwdriver and told them to bring it on. It was a vicious fight in the darkness, with everyone slashing at arms and legs without quite knowing whose, but the upshot of it was that Joe ended up in the Northern General for eight weeks with serious internal injuries, and when he came out the only army he would have been good for was the Salvos.

When Davey heard about what had gone on, he wanted to go and run Shelley Turner and Mark Crabbe over and then reverse back over their twitching remains, but Jasmine told him not to be such a hot-headed twat. So he had a couple of cans of Strongbow to calm down, and then called Karamat and whinged to him about it. Karamat made all the right noises of sympathy in his thick accent, but it was obvious he wasn't going to lift a finger. What did it have to do with him?

So Davey called on his old mate Navid, who had driven one of Arshan's taxis and lived next door to Joe's family.

'Those poor bastards,' said Nav. 'He had his whole life ahead of him, and now it's ruined. You try to earn an honest day's pay and something like this happens.' He was scratching away on a scratchcard as he said it. Nav was mad on scratchcards. He had won a grand once, and spent it on a Bose sound system.

Davey said that mad buggers like Shelley Turner and Mark Crabbe needed to be taught a lesson, and Nav agreed.

After Shelley Turner's dad died, her older sister Tyler had taken her in, because it was pretty clear that if she stayed on her own she would drink herself to death before the year was out. Tyler lived with her partner Craig and two kids Dillon and Jodie on a beige-rendered semi in the next estate. It was a bit more upmarket, with the odd owner-occupier and a few student houses. The local sandwich shop sold feta and roasted vegetable wraps.

Jodie moved in to share with Dillon, and Shelley got her room. It was a bit weird walking in to this pink bedroom with clouds and Barbies, and seeing ashtrays and empty WKD bottles balanced everywhere. At first Shelley behaved herself pretty well, and although she was drinking a lot and coming in late, Tyler said that people dealt with death in different ways. Craig said, as long she didn't wake him when he was on night shift, it was fine for now.

Then she got a bit more erratic, coming in from nights out while the kids were eating breakfast and swearing and breathing vodka fumes all over their mini shredded wheats. She was all girly and sweet with Jodie but Jodie said it scared her sometimes, and she wasn't ready to wear clothes like that. Shelley swore a lot in front of Dillon and told him he was trouble, and once he said that she pinched his leg really hard, but there was no one else there to see it and Shelley said he was making it up because she caught him poking around her dirty knickers. Tyler said that was another thing, it wouldn't hurt to do her own laundry and keep Jodie's room a bit tidier, would it?

'My room,' said Shelley, exhaling smoke in a thick long plume.

The neighbours said that grief was one thing, but it was a wonder Tyler, and especially Craig, put up with Shelley for so long. But Mim at number 56 opposite said that she had happened to glance across through the front bedroom window and seen Craig porking Shelley from behind one day when Tyler was out at work, so now Shelley had something over Craig and he couldn't say shit.

But when Shelley came back after that night up the allot-ments with blood all over her arms and a look in her eye like she'd just had a line of coke with the devil himself, and Mark Crabbe was rolling around in the hydrangea sobbing for them to take him to hospital, Tyler had had enough. Craig spread a bin bag on the passenger seat of the Passat and drove Mark to the Northern General. 'Leave him at the gates,' said Tyler. 'Don't stay with the prick.' Meanwhile, Tyler gave Shelley a mug of tea and five Nytol, and put her to sleep in the garden shed.

In the morning Tyler ran Shelley a bath while Craig drove the kids over to his mother's. Tyler said Shelley had to go away or Davey Wilson and the Turkish connection would be down there with baseball bats and petrol bombs, and Tyler wasn't having Dillon and Jodie traumatised by seeing their psycho auntie raped or cut up or worse in front of them. So she bought Shelley a single to London and put her on the train, and told her to stay with their Uncle Max or that ex-boyfriend of hers or someone, but get some help, or go out on the game and get murdered in sodding Soho for all she cared.

On the train was a lad called Gareth Slater, who had played Sunday league football with Joe and was on his way down to Leicester for the Wednesday game. He had heard about what had happened. When he saw Shelley he started giving her the evil eye and then flinging insults down the carriage like 'slut' and 'evil bitch' and so on and so forth. Shelley discreetly gave him the rods, but stayed quiet, and got the waterworks going so that when the conductor came in she said Gareth was abusing her, the others passengers backed her up, and Gareth was asked to leave the train in Derby and met for a stern word by the British Transport Police.

13

A FEW WEEKS after the dust had settled, Aidan turned up back in Sheffy. Everyone had heard about his scrapes up north, and everyone had an opinion, that he was either a legend or a bell-end, according to their point of view.

Irene who manned the phones at the taxi office said the sooner he ended up dead in a ditch the more peaceful life would be for everyone else. But Gemma, who had only been there six weeks and had all the drivers eating out of her hand, said it was young men like Aidan that made her proud to be British.

Davey was glad that Aidan had got to know Ryan, and although he wouldn't go so far as to say that he had missed him, he met him off the train and welcomed him back by taking him to a pub on London Road for a pint of Stones. By this time Nick had a good job as a precision toolmaker, and he came down and joined them after work and it was happy families.

When Aidan heard about what had happened to Joe, he was all for hunting down Shelley and Mark and giving them a pasting.

Davey laughed. 'Alright junior. Let's wait till your balls have dropped.'

Aidan was fuming at that, but Nick said it didn't matter anyway as Shelley had cleared off down south and Mark was nowhere to be found.

At tennish Davey wobbled off home and Aidan and Nick went on to West Street, and then to some club that had started up since he was away, and kept on drinking.

Some of the lads who Aidan had known when he was younger were in the club, all a bit bigger and older, including that Foxy who he had had a fight with behind the incinerator that time. Foxy was a swimming instructor now. He helped out at the special school and was generally thought of as a rare commodity.

Aidan remembered that the last time they'd met, Foxy had split his lip, and sat in the throbbing darkness of the club brooding over his Jägerbomb. It had never been decided which of them was the hardest. He waited till Foxy went to the toilets, followed him in and jogged his arm while he was trying to piss.

'What's the matter with you, you knob?' said Foxy. 'What do you want?'

'I want a fight.'

'Alright, well, let me finish my piss first.'

Aidan pushed him again, so Foxy turned round and sprayed wee at him, getting it all over Aidan's trousers and shoes. Aidan stood there speechless for a moment, which gave Foxy time to put his cock away, and then they started trading punches right there in the nightclub bogs. Other lads came in, saw what was happening and either went away again or stood there egging them on, and it didn't take long for a crowd to form. Aidan and Foxy were both slithering about on the tiles that were slippy with other men's piss, trying to get at each other but unable to stand up or find room for a proper swing.

Ian the bouncer, who had gone to school with Davey way back, came in and burst out laughing at them.

'Get up, you silly pricks,' he said. 'What are you arguing about? Who's got the biggest knob?'

'I don't even know,' said Foxy. 'He's off his head.'

'It's just a bit of fun,' said Aidan, dusting himself down.

'It doesn't look much fun to me,' said Ian. 'Look Aidan, Foxy's a good lad. Leave him alone, eh? He doesn't need your crap.'

Aidan agreed. Then Ian said he'd have to chuck them out because they had been fighting, but the club was about to close anyway, so Aidan and Foxy went to get a burger with cheese sauce from the van and patched up their differences. Then Foxy went home, but Aidan hung about outside the club till Ian came out.

'Hey up, Ian,' he said. 'I hear you're off on a fishing trip in a few weeks. I might come along, show you how it's done.'

'Aye, alright,' said Ian. It was the end of a long night and he wanted to get home. But as they went their separate ways, he turned back and said, 'I'll have to ask my mate Terry if there's room for you, though. He's the best man.'

'Whatever,' said Aidan. 'I would have thought that the stag could invite who he liked, but if you need to ask Terry's permission then go ahead. See what your fiancée thinks too – and her mother. It'll be good practice for getting under the thumb.'

Ian let this go because Aidan was pissed and he wasn't, and said he'd be in touch to let him know if he could come, and then said something else under his breath.

14

NICK AND HIS mates were having a PGA Golf session on the Wii. It was happening at Carl's house and there would be two four-balls running simultaneously on two tellies. It was going to take all weekend, and even that might be pushing it because Carl's girlfriend Louise was coming from Manchester with a sheet of acid.

As it turned out, Louise tried some of the acid on the TransPennine Express, and had to call Carl to drive over and pick her up from Edale station where the kids from *The Wicker Man* had her hemmed in by some wheelie bins. When they got back Carl took her up to bed. He always liked screwing her when she was off her face. Then he left her to sleep it off and came down for the game, but it meant they were a player short. So Nick called Aidan.

'An evening with the golf spods,' said Aidan. 'How can I resist?'

But the truth was he was at a loose end. Davey and Jasmine were settling down to 9½ *Weeks* with a bottle of Aldi Rioja, and he didn't fancy lying awake later listening to the bump-bump of the headboard as Davey gave his mum the Mickey Rourke treatment. So he said he'd be round.

'No fighting, though,' said Nick. But Aidan had already put the phone down.

When he got there, the air was thick with the smell of skunk and spilt lager. As well as Nick and Carl and Connor and Foxy, there was Lisa, Connor's girlfriend, and her redhead mate, and Jordan Smith, a badmouthed little scrote from Aidan's year who fancied himself as an MC, and had gone around telling people that the reason Aidan had stayed in Newcastle all that time was because Davey wasn't his real dad and had said he wasn't welcome. Aidan knew all about it, but he never mentioned it to Jordan.

By the time they were setting off on the back nine, the wheels were starting to come off the golf cart. They would all sit around in a haze until someone said, 'Whose go is it?' and whoever it was would lurch to his feet and try to swing the controller. Aidan was five shots off the lead, but he didn't give a toss about that. He was more interested in giving Lisa's mate the eye.

When Jordan stood up for his tee shot on the tenth, he had his back to where Aidan was sitting, and he let out a massive guff right in Aidan's face. It really stank, but Aidan gave no reaction other than a little frown. But when Jordan was lining up his shot, waggling the controller about like he was Tiger Woods, Aidan lifted his leg and gave him a shove right in the arse with his foot. Jordan went flying forwards into the telly and sent it on to the floor. The screen smashed. Aidan and Lisa and Lisa's redhead mate were laughing their heads off, but all the others were going, 'Fucking hell,' and waving their arms in the air and shouting. Jordan looked round from where he was tangled up on the floor with the Wii and the telly cables, but he saw Aidan standing over him and decided not to get up.

That was the end of the game, so they all fucked off in twos and threes to find somewhere safe to recover from the acid and bitch about each other. Nick was quiet on the way home, but Aidan kept chortling to himself. 'What's she called, Lisa's mate?' he kept asking, but as soon as Nick told him he kept forgetting the answer, and when they got back he fell asleep on a chair in the kitchen.

Davey was on the sofa. 'I can't work her out,' he said, meaning Jasmine. 'I only asked—'

'I don't want to know,' said Nick.

'What are you doing back, anyway?'

'Ask Mr Mental,' said Nick, and starting skinning up.

'Fuck's sake,' said Davey.

15

THERE WAS A guy called Karol who ran a car wash on the A61 north out of the city. He had been a weightlifter back in Poland, but when he ruptured his Achilles tendon they heard the snap in Vilnius, and now he had come to England to sell steroids to grunts and shag Jordan Smith's sister Teagan. Teagan was about half his height and built like a china doll, and it seemed wrong for them to be doing it even though she was nearly eighteen.

Karol had these other Polish guys working for him at the car wash, Sebastian who had been a lorry driver till his epilepsy got too bad, and Daniel who was a computer programmer and much more of a weed, but always made these sarcastic remarks in Polish that made the others crack up.

Teagan was mates with Connor's girlfriend Lisa and her redhead friend, whose name was Ashleigh, and this meant that Connor ended up spending a bit of time with the Polish lads. He said they weren't so bad, and not half so annoying as that Louise his brother was going out with, who half the time was vegged out on acid and half the time was wearing black lipstick and going on about jazz and Third Wave Feminism.

One day Jasmine got a call from Martin the car salesman to say that Aidan's sister Amy was off the rails again, so Nick and Aidan caught a bus on the Saturday and went to see them in their Barratt home. When they got there Amy was paralytic and the house was awash with half-bottles of vodka, most of them empty. But it turned out that what Martin really meant when he said that Amy was going off the rails again was that she had been sharing a pair of knickers with little Daniel from the car wash, who would drive her out to the woods in the rust-bucket Audi TT which Martin had sold him and ply her with plum moonshine till she opened up. Sometimes she was gone for days on end. Now Martin was cursing Connor for introducing him and Amy to the Polish boys. When she was at home he had started locking her in the house, and it was the cabin fever that was really sending her doolally.

'It's no business of mine who she's shagging,' said Aidan, when Martin had put him in the picture. 'It seems to me you're the psycho.' He said that if Martin kept Amy locked in the house any more he'd come back and rearrange Martin's face.

But Nick got on the phone to Connor, and Connor said that Lisa had been talking to Teagan and Karol had said to Teagan that Daniel had been bragging about how he was screwing Amy, saying she was an alky slut and if any of the others fancied coming along next time they could have a go too. Aidan sat there with a worried furrow on his brow, and said that it wasn't just that he couldn't have that, it was knowing that Karol and Teagan and Lisa and Connor all knew about it and God knew who else, probably that Ashleigh he liked, and he didn't like the idea of her hearing that sort of shit about him and his family.

So they waited till Amy woke up and told her what Connor had said, that Daniel and all the other Poles were laughing at her, and although it was probably just the remorse from the booze, she cried and said she knew Daniel was a prick and Martin was the only one who could save her and all the usual tripe. Nick said he and Aidan would deal with Daniel, but she had to promise to give up the booze.

'I will,' she said. 'I so will. This time I really mean it.' But they didn't even bother to reply.

On the way home Aidan and Nick called in at the car wash and Aidan put a brick through the Audi's windscreen, and Karol, Sebastian and Daniel, plus Jordan Smith and some middle-aged dude with a pock-marked face and a car jack in his hand, all chased them down the road towards the football stadium.

The upshot was that Aidan and Nick had made enemies of the car-wash Poles, Amy would probably go back to Daniel as soon as she felt miserable enough, Connor was pissed off at getting caught in the middle, and Teagan and Lisa were probably telling Ashleigh how much trouble Aidan was and how she'd be better off with Sebastian.

'Jesus Christ,' said Irene at the taxi office, exhaling a thick jet of fag smoke up at an angle. 'Bring back national service, I say.' And she called through to Brendan to pick her up a mince and onion pie.

16

IAN THE BARMAN met his mate Terry for a swift couple in some dire sports bar in Hillsborough. The truth was, Ian was finding Penny a bit full-on about the wedding. It was like she went into deputy-head mode and started setting him assignments. She said her first husband, Dave, had always been too busy to talk about the things she wanted to talk about, and Ian began to wonder if he had made a tactical mistake. He'd liked it better when she was gasping into his ear about feeling sixteen again.

Terry couldn't help with any of that crap. But he was keen to firm up the arrangements for the stag do. Terry worked for the city council and used phrases like 'firm up' all the time.

'Are we still a man short?' said Ian. 'I saw that Aidan Wilson the other night and he was up for it.'

'Christ,' said Terry. 'A mad kid. Haven't you got any other real friends? What about whatsisname, from Barnsley?'

'He's not as bad as all that. He'll liven things up a bit.'

'No. Fucking. Way,' said Terry, and Ian could see that he had a point.

So they all went off on the minibus to Anglesey, Ian and Terry and Tony the builder and no end of middle-aged blokes, with an empty seat at the back where they stacked three crates of beer.

When Aidan heard they'd gone without him he was furious. He found out when they were due back and went and waited in the car park of Asda, which was the drop-off point.

They all stumbled off the bus, tired and hungover and still a bit sicky after thirteen hours on a rough sea. Ian saw Aidan waiting and said there was going to be trouble. Sure enough, he came straight up and started effing and blinding, calling them knobs and asking them what the fuck they thought they were doing, and squaring up to Ian ready to fight.

'Oh, put your cock away,' said Ian. 'I know you've made a bit of name for yourself, but I've seen more young bucks go sprawling on the pavement than you've had hot dinners. And so have these lot. So shut your mouth and fuck off, or we'll beat the shit out of you.'

And all these balding hard men fronted up to Aidan, a dozen sunburnt beer bellies covered with grubby polo shirts.

Aidan couldn't help clenching his fists and for a minute it seemed like he would attack them anyway, but then he turned and walked off towards the park without saying anything. When he got home Nick asked him what had happened, and Aidan said, 'I'm not such a stupid bastard as to get myself killed.' He tried to laugh it off, but the truth was that it rankled inside him that he hadn't been able to take on big Ian in a straight fight, and from then on he was always watching out for some kind of nasty trouble that he could prove himself in. Between being laughed at by old men, Joe from down the road having his stomach cut open, and a little Polish weasel shagging his sister, there was a lot of anger he was looking to get out.

17

AIDAN AND DAVEY were getting on worse than ever, and Aidan spent half the time kipping on the sofa at Nick's place. It was a flat over a Chinese, handy for town, and in the summer nights it was good to lean out the window and chuck eggs at the drunks. In the mornings when Nick left for the works, Aidan would get up and work on the hole he was making behind the dartboard to spy on the people next door. It was like *The Great Escape*, only instead of putting the dust in his pockets and sprinkling it down his trouser legs, he just dumped it in the toilet and gave it a flush. He figured if the drains got blocked, Nick's landlord would have to pay.

It wasn't that the woman next door was a particular looker. It was just something to do. He had a vague idea that he could find out details of their lives and then mess with their heads by leaving presents on the doorstep, or whatever. But it turned out that the wall was a bit thicker than he'd hoped, and he never made the breakthrough. When Nick eventually found out about what he was doing, he gave Aidan this long, weird look as if to say he wasn't right in the head.

One time he said, 'You know you cut off the end of that teacher's knob . . . And remember the flasher . . .' Then he got embarrassed, and it was a relief when Aidan said, 'I'm not gay, if that's what you mean,' even though that wasn't what he'd meant at all.

Aidan would head up home to see Jasmine in the afternoons

when Davey would most likely have gone to the pub or the bookies. But this one time he knew before he got through the front door that Davey was still at home because he could hear him and Jasmine rowing like there was no tomorrow.

At least Davey had never been the sort of cunt to knock a woman about. Although there was that time that Jasmine lost a tooth falling out of the social club pissed. Aidan hadn't been there, and they could tell you anything, couldn't they? But Jasmine did tend to get carried away with the rum and cokes. Like the time she had called Irene a stale old cow and whacked her with a pizza box.

Anyway, Davey wasn't knocking her black and blue. In fact it was Jasmine who was the angry one. It turned out that what they were arguing about was the dirty texts that she had discovered on Davey's phone from some tart called Michelle. First he said that they were from a wrong number, then he said that this Michelle was a crazy bitch and she was stalking him. 'It's all in her head,' he said, probably imagining himself as Clint Eastwood in *Play Misty for Me*. Then he made out it was Greg the tobacco smuggler winding him up. He was like a worm on a hook. 'In more ways than one,' said Jasmine.

Eventually she got it out of him that Michelle was the trainee hairdresser at the Last Chance Salon and he had been boning her on the quiet for the last six months.

'How old is she anyway?' said Jasmine while Davey was wiping a dishcloth over the scratches on his face.

He said, 'About twenty,' which meant eighteen tops.

Jasmine was blazing away about how she was going to smash this Michelle's head in, but she had nearly run out of steam when Aidan turned up. He got the story out of them and then had Davey up against the kitchen cabinets with a bread knife.

There was a stand-off then, with Aidan screwing his face up and pushing his eyes out on stalks, Jasmine begging him to let Davey go and Davey telling him he was a mad little bastard and he should listen to his mother. It was only when Jay, who at that stage was about eleven years old, came in to get himself a bowl of Frosties and Aidan saw the shock on his face that he put the knife down and let Davey off with a couple of hard punches in the stomach. Then Davey was sprawled all over the lino coughing and retching and Jasmine was lighting up a Lambert and Jay was putting his little puffa jacket on and saying he'd go out for chips. Jasmine gave him a couple of quid from her purse. Aidan stood by the draining board picking up mugs and wanging them into the corner one after another.

'I really thought you were going to do it,' said Jasmine afterwards, looking at Aidan with these weird flashing eyes. If she hadn't been his mother he might have said she was up for it, but as it was he felt like Mark Crabbe with Shelley Turner egging him on to shove a screwdriver into some kid.

'I will do next time,' he said, looking at Davey. But Davey was too busy trying to get a bottle of Beefeater to his lips without spilling it. 'We'll have to buy some new fucking mugs, now,' said Aidan, staring at Davey like that was the worst thing about what had happened.

18

A SHLEIGH THE REDHEAD worked on the tills at Aldi, and she took it dead seriously. She wouldn't pass bottles of cider down the belt without scanning them, even for Lisa or her uncle Jim. When Aidan found out where she worked, he used to go down there and buy an orange or a half-litre bottle of soy sauce, just so he could say hi and have a gander at her tits jutting out under the nylon smock.

They would smile at each other for a few seconds, and then Ashleigh would start on the next person's shopping and Aidan would walk off, and they would look at each other again, still smiling but kind of sad in the eyes this time. On the way home Aidan threw the orange over someone's garden wall, and he was angry and glad at the same time.

Gradually they got more confident with each other, started saying hello and so on, just small talk that meant, 'I haven't got anything to say but I like you.' If it was quiet he would hang around the till and make stupid jokes, and she would make a face like, 'That was a shit joke but I'm laughing anyway.' But he never plucked up the courage to ask her out, and it started to seem like that was there things between them would end.

Then one day when Aidan had gone in for a can of Red Bull, Ashleigh said, 'Can I see you later? I need your help.'

It was obvious from the way she asked that it wasn't exactly a come-on. But Aidan agreed to come back at the end of her shift.

In the mean time he went home and had a shower, sprayed himself all over including the underside of his balls with deodorant, and went into the toilet of the Duke of Norfolk where there was a condom machine you could get to give out for free with a sharp whack on the side.

Ashleigh was waiting outside the shop with a Gola top over her uniform.

'You're really fit,' said Aidan, and she smiled.

They went to the park and sat on the swings and she told him about all the shit that was going on that she didn't know what to do about. She said, Lisa and Teagan were no use, they were just silly girls, and everyone else she knew thought *she* was a silly girl and they would just laugh it off. But she had heard about Aidan chopping that pervert's knob off in Newcastle and maybe he would understand.

Ashleigh had been living with her uncle Jim again, after her mum died. It wasn't that big of a deal, because her mum had been in and out of hospital, using and trying not to, her whole life. So it was more like your nan dying really, someone weak and old who you loved but didn't rely on.

Jim drove a minicab in Rotherham. He said it was easier pickings out there than in the city centre. Plus, he was having an affair with a forty-year-old granny in Mexborough, so it made sense to be out that way in case she called to say the coast was clear. Her bloke went fishing at a pond that was only down the road, so you had to be in and out pretty quickly. With the driving and the Wednesday season ticket and the benders at the weekends, Ashleigh didn't see him much. She had the house to herself, but instead of inviting everyone round to sit drinking voddy and sniffing coke and wrecking the place, like Lisa or Teagan or anyone normal would have done, she just looked after the place and got on with her GCSE resits and working at the supermarket, and went out with Lisa on a Friday and a Saturday night. She did Jim's washing. Once, she even washed the curtains. She bought the food. She told Lisa Jim was a bit of a misery and didn't want anyone coming round, which was true, but she didn't tell her that he was never there, so it didn't matter.

'Has he been knocking you about?' said Aidan, but Ashleigh said, 'Jim? No. He's alright. Just doesn't like anyone under thirty.'

But sitting in the empty house all day, struggling over her textbooks, Ashleigh had started to hear some pretty dodgy things from the house next door.

When she had been staying with Jim before, years back, there had been a family living there, a woman called Danielle who worked in a sandwich shop and a man called Brett who worked in a big customer services call centre out by the M1. They had an eight-year-old, Paige, who Ashleigh used to play with a bit, and a toddler called Poppy. Danielle used to lean over the garden fence and ask Ashleigh if she was OK, what with her mum being 'ill' and having to live with her uncle who meant well but hadn't really got a clue. And Ashleigh used to say yes, because she had a telly in her own room and there were plenty of fish fingers for breakfast, dinner and tea.

But while she was living with her mum again, things had changed. Brett was long gone, and Paige had moved out a year or two earlier. Danielle had this new bloke, Gary Lamb. He was a suit. He drove a newish Honda Accord which he used to take empty bottles to the bottle bank. He and Danielle and Poppy were probably going to move to a nicer area, but it was just talk as yet. Danielle didn't work at the sandwich shop any more. Poppy was eleven or twelve now, and she was dead quiet, like a little ghost.

What Ashleigh had heard through the wall was hard to say. It wasn't the usual bust-ups that went on in everyone's house sooner or later, raised voices and that – or the smashing glass, shouts and screams that said a man was knocking a woman about. Anyway Danielle never had any bruises, none that you could see on her face and arms. It was something else, something quieter and worse. It was a lot of crying. 'A lot,' Ashleigh said again emphatically, looking Aidan in the face, then down again at her feet dangling from the swing. It was Poppy crying, and sometimes when Danielle was out of the house a low man's voice barely rumbling through the wall, creepy like, 'and then – you know, moaning and groaning, like, and sex sounds – like he's getting excited, or coming, or whatever.' When Danielle was out. Like, did Aidan think it could be what she thought it was?

Ashleigh had tried to ask Poppy about it, but she'd just put on a dead face and walked off, and then she'd asked Danielle, who had put on a face like Ashleigh didn't know what, waves of rage and fuck off and horror and panic like a bad things rainbow, and then she'd shut her face and shut the door, and Ashleigh hadn't seen her since.

'I'm thinking this is why Paige moved out,' she said.

'Fuck,' said Aidan, but he didn't say anything else for a while.

They went to the house. Jim was out in the taxi and would be off granny-shagging for a couple of days, because her husband was going to Dublin for a monster truck and Guinness weekend. They listened at the wall, and then went into the back garden and Aidan scoped out the house, but it was just a shit Sheffield terrace like all the rest. Ashleigh made spaghetti hoops on toast and they drank Carling and watched one of Jim's old war films. Then Ashleigh went to bed. Aidan slept on the sofa, and although he had been with Ashleigh all evening, watching her face and getting the occasional waft of how she smelt, he didn't toss himself off, because it didn't feel right.

The next morning, they waited until Gary drove off, and then Aidan hopped over the fence and walked in the open back door, and Ashleigh followed. Danielle was washing up and Poppy was eating own-brand coco pops. Aidan just stood leaning against the worktop and didn't say anything, and with him there backing her up Ashleigh went into overdrive. She said they weren't going to be palmed off and she knew Gary was doing some disgusting things and they were going to stop him, and it was OK for Danielle and Poppy to admit it. She talked for a long time with Danielle stood there with suds on her hands saying nothing or sometimes no, and sometimes, get out of my house, what are you doing in my kitchen. But Ashleigh said they wouldn't go and looked across at Aidan who didn't say anything but just nodded and kept standing there so she could keep talking. Danielle kept saying no, that was all lies and Ashleigh had it wrong, but then Aidan said, 'Are you in on it, then?' and she went quiet. And then Ashleigh said all nice to Poppy, 'Is it true, does he do things to you?' and Poppy sat looking down into her bowl of brown milk for a long time and they all held their breath and then she nodded.

Danielle collapsed into sobbing and sat on the kitchen floor, so Aidan got her a glass of water while Ashleigh kept on talking to Poppy. She asked her what exactly Gary had done, and Aidan didn't want to listen to the answers but knew that if he left the room the spell would be broken.

Poppy said sometimes he filmed it on his phone and made her watch it with him again later on his computer.

'You can't call the police,' said Danielle.

Ashleigh opened her mouth to speak but before she could, Aidan said, 'We're not going to.'

Ashleigh said, 'We fucking are,' and then there was a stand-off because Danielle was starting to say no again and Poppy didn't look like she could say yes without her mum. So Ashleigh said they would take these videos off Gary's computer and then they would have the evidence even if it took Danielle and Poppy a few days to decide to go to the police.

Danielle said they would have to be quick because Gary might be back soon. Aidan picked up a kitchen knife off the draining board and put it in his pocket.

On the way upstairs Ashleigh said under her breath, 'We'll go to the police anyway.'

Aidan didn't say anything.

19

UPSTAIRS, THEY FOUND the computer in the spare room with an exercise bike and a folded-up ironing board. They booted it up and Aidan started looking around. Ashleigh said, 'Do a search for video files,' but Aidan didn't know how to do that so he stood up to let her do it. She found some files. But before Ashleigh could play one, Aidan said, 'Hadn't you better go downstairs and make sure they're OK?'

She looked at him. They both listened, and heard nothing. Ashleigh went downstairs to see what was happening.

Aidan played the first of the videos. It was of Poppy, fully clothed, sitting on the sofa watching telly. She looked sad, but nothing happened. Aidan dragged the slider on. It was just fifteen minutes of the same thing. He closed the file and opened another one at random.

This one was different. And worse.

It was Poppy, naked, standing by a bed. Then a man's voice ordering her to do things, go into various poses, and her doing what he said. Then basically Gary walking into shot and raping her.

Aidan stood watching the screen. He didn't stop the video or move the slider. He just stood and watched every second. He didn't want to see it but he couldn't stop watching, wanting to throw up, as this man did those things to the little girl. All the time he was thinking, 'I don't want to have seen this,' but he kept watching. On Poppy, he saw the dead face which

Ashleigh had talked about, and on the man he saw private eyes like nothing existed for Gary Lamb except himself. He was dimly aware of a noise downstairs where Ashleigh was dealing with Poppy and Danielle, and knew that he should be stopping the video and copying the files on to Ashleigh's Hello Kitty USB drive, but he couldn't help but watch until the end, when Gary moved back out of shot and there was just Poppy lying whimpering on the bed.

He was about to start copying the files when he felt a blow to the base of his skull and fell forwards into the computer. His vision closed in to a tiny dot and he knew that if it reached total blackness he would pass out and then probably end up dead. He had time to put out his hand and steady himself on the flimsy Ikea desk and half-turn to ward off the second blow, which caught him flush in the middle of his forearm and made a crack like it broke it.

Then Gary kicked him in the face and Aidan felt his lip ripping and saw a couple of teeth ping out towards the exercise bike. He found himself thinking for an instant that he would have to go down on his hands and knees searching for them in the carpet.

It was a steering lock that Gary was battering him with. He was raising it again, and Aidan was trying to get up off his arse to dodge out of the way and trying to tell Gary he was a fucking cunt at the same time, but he knew that there was just a splurge of noise, blood and spittle coming out his mouth and he could barely get his body into a crouching position.

The wheel lock smacked into the side of his face. As well as the pain, which certainly really fucking hurt, his whole face felt floppy, and he supposed that Gary had broken his jaw. He slumped down on the floor by the desk and he could see everything starting to go black again, and Gary was grinning and prowling round the room like he was half enjoying the moment and half not knowing what to do next.

'Been enjoying my videos, have you?'

The blackness had nearly closed altogether. It was like he was watching what was going on through a toilet roll.

'Maybe you'd rather have a look at the real thing.'

Gary paced over and gave him another kick, a half-arsed one but hard enough to make his vision go completely. He wasn't sure if he actually passed out or just stopped thinking for a bit, but then he heard a noise and managed to open his eyes again. Gary was pulling Poppy into the room by her arm. She looked shit scared. She was looking at Aidan, and he knew that the reason she was so scared was because she knew that the usual thing was going to happen, but it was going to be even worse, and maybe she was going to die.

'Here you are then fella,' said Gary. 'A live show.'

Gary was unbuckling his belt and undoing his flies. While he was doing it, Poppy just kind of stood there waiting.

As well as the massive pain in his arm and all over his face and the back of his head, Aidan realised that the side of his thigh fucking hurt as well. That was when he remembered about the knife in his pocket.

The arm on that side of his body was the broken one, but there was nothing else for it. Gary wasn't watching him now – he had got his stiff dick out and was starting to waggle it in his stepdaughter's direction. Aidan made his arm move round towards his trouser pocket. All the time it was hurting like someone had lit a firework under his skin.

He thought, if I can manage to do this then I know I can put up with anything.

He got a weak grip on the end of the knife handle and slid it an inch or two out of his pocket, where the other hand could reach it. There was a lot of blood gathered under him, and he wondered if he'd cut an artery in his leg. He glanced up at Gary, but he wasn't thinking about Aidan any more, he was starting to do his vile things. So Aidan reached across his body and picked up the knife in his left hand, braced his foot on the floor and forced himself up towards them.

He didn't have much strength. He pushed the knife into Gary's belly and then collapsed on to his knees in front of him, holding on to the paedo's suit jacket to keep himself up. Gary gasped and stood there looking down at him and at his own knob suddenly no longer so stiff. He didn't seem injured, just surprised, so Aidan pulled the knife out and pushed it in again, aiming up under the ribs a bit more this time. He felt Gary crumple backwards a bit, so he pulled the knife out and stabbed him again, and again, and they slowly fell back in heap against the far wall of the room, Gary still letting out a long breathless gasp and Aidan limply stabbing and withdrawing the knife until Gary's belly was cut to ribbons and gushing blood, and the fall was over and the gasp was ended.

Aidan looked round and saw Poppy standing watching the pair of them. She didn't seem in the least interested. She didn't have the dead face now, just completely neutral.

'Get Ashleigh, get your mum,' Aidan tried to say, and although it came out as a bubbly groan of agony, she turned and ran off out of the room. Aidan heard the *thud-thud* of her footsteps getting quieter on the stairs.

20

As it turned out, Poppy couldn't get Ashleigh and her mum because they were padlocked into the downstairs bog. So she walked out into the street and bumped into a BT engineer, and he came in and heard them shouting, ran upstairs where Poppy was pointing and saw Aidan and Gary and said 'Oh my God,' called the police and the ambulance, and then got his toolbox out the van and broke open the toilet to let Ashleigh and Danielle out. The side of Ashleigh's face had swelled up like a watermelon where Gary had belted her. But as she said afterwards, it could have been a fuck of a lot worse.

Aidan had a broken jaw and a broken ulna, a broken nose and four missing teeth, a deep cut to his tongue, a deeper one to the back of his thigh, moderate-to-severe bruising, and a fracture at the base of his skull which healed fine in a couple of months but could just as easily have killed him. His whole body hurt to fuck. He didn't mind that. It was like the ache in a marathon runner's legs after they've won the race.

What he did mind was how he would be lying in the hospital bed and see the video again playing out in his mind whether his eyes were open or shut. It would flash up in front of him while he was eating breakfast or while the consultant was trying to talk to him about his injuries. At night what he had seen would keep him from getting to sleep, and then when he did finally drop off he would dream about it. He would dream that he was lying on the floor of the spare room and this time he didn't have the strength to get to the knife and so he would have to watch while Gary did what he was doing, and then Gary would strangle Poppy and turn to Aidan to kill him too and that's when Aidan would wake up.

The doctors said it had been a tremendous shock and things would calm down in time when Aidan's brain had had a chance to digest everything, but if that didn't happen then he might have to do some therapy to help it.

'Like the squaddies when they come back from Iraq,' said Ashleigh.

But maybe Aidan's brain wasn't good at digesting things, because for the whole of the rest of his life Aidan never liked being alone. Whenever he was alone the video and the events in the spare room came back to him and played over and over in his mind and made all sorts of horrible thoughts occur to him, as if his brain was saying that if it had to remember that then it would try to think of other things just to see if there was anything worse.

After he had recovered enough to be out of danger Aidan was remanded in custody. Because of all the videos and the evidence that Danielle and Ashleigh gave, he was only charged with manslaughter. He would probably have got off altogether with a suspended sentence, except for three things that the Crown prosecutor pointed out.

One, if it was self-defence then why had he put a kitchen knife in his pocket before he went upstairs?

Two, why had he told police he had found the knife on the floor of the spare room when both Ashleigh and Danielle had seen him pick it up in the kitchen?

And three, if it was self-defence then why had he stabbed Mr Lamb twenty-seven times, when he could have been reasonably sure that he was completely incapacitated and probably fatally injured after four or five?

Aidan said, 'So if I'd stopped stabbing him after he was dead then I'd have got off? I'm going down because I stabbed a corpse?'

And his solicitor said, 'Yes.'

Plus he was mixed race of course.

The barristers went round the houses for a good long while, but the upshot of it was that even though he had pleaded guilty, Aidan got four years.

21

ALL THE TIME Aidan was on remand, stories were going round the estate about what had gone on. Most people said that Aidan was a hero. Half the blokes said they would have done the same thing themselves, but then their wives and girlfriends put on *yeah, right* faces as if they'd just claimed to have a twelve-inch cock. People would stop at the checkout and say to Ashleigh, 'You must be dead proud of your Aidan,' and she knew they must think that she and Aidan were an item, even though they weren't.

'We haven't done it, anyway,' she said to Lisa.

But she couldn't say to people, 'He's not *my* Aidan,' because that would look like she wasn't proud of him. Plus, she wasn't going to start explaining the details in the middle of Aldi either, it wasn't any of their chuffing business, so she would just smile and nod.

She visited him, though, and it was sort of settled between them, without either of them saying it, that if he hadn't been inside then they'd have been going out with each other. She had a dream where she was brave enough to say in the visiting room, 'Oh, I want you so much,' and then they were in a bedroom that was sort of her cousin Dean's but not, and they were doing it, but after a bit Aidan turned into Antony Costa from Blue, and then she woke up with stomach ache and had to go to the bathroom to look for a tampon.

Ashleigh heard from Teagan that Karol and Sebastian were

impressed with what Aidan had done to Gary Lamb. They said he had bollocks. But that prick Daniel who had been shagging Aidan's sister Amy said there was something fishy about it. He said that Gary had probably only attacked Aidan because he found him wanking over his videos, or more likely they had agreed that Aidan could 'have a go' on Poppy and then Gary had got jealous and changed his mind.

Teagan said no one listened to any of that shit and Karol had said Daniel should shut his mouth, but he kept making out to random people that Aidan was a paedo. Even though he did it in a jokey way, everyone agreed that Daniel was a bit of a silly bastard and his gob was going to land him in trouble. And then one night he had a bit too much to drink and wrapped his Audi round an old man, and he was up in court himself.

22

JASMINE AND NICK were there in court on the day Aidan was sentenced. So was Amy, but she disappeared to the pub at lunchtime and didn't come back. Kayla, Aidan's other sister, was used to court and so on from her Stephen being a serial offender, and even though they hadn't seen each other for four years she called out 'Alright Aid' across the court to him and made a clenched fist that meant 'Stay strong' or summat like that.

Aidan's little brother Jay was nearly twelve now, and he came to court with a black jumper on to show respect, and sat with Jasmine and played on his PSP. But when he saw Aidan looking at him he grinned like he was on an accumulator at Donny races and gave him the thumbs up.

Davey hadn't come, not that Aidan expected him to. While Aidan was on remand Jasmine had been sacked from her cleaning job at the care home for swearing at the residents, so she had come home early, and found Davey shagging his mate Dwayne's sister Rikki. Rikki was Jasmine's best mate on the estate. So for the last four weeks Davey and Rikki had been shacked up at Dwayne's while Rikki's boyfriend Jason stood outside the front door shouting the odds and Dwayne shouted back that they weren't there and fuck off as well. Jasmine had sent Davey a text saying when Aidan's sentencing was 'if ur bothered', but it wasn't a massive surprise that he was lying low.

The gallery was full of other people, some of them Aidan's friends and people off the estate and some of them strangers, all mad keen to show support for Aidan for killing the pervert. On the front row sort of with Aidan's family and sort of on her own was Ashleigh, sitting all still and serious, and next to her Danielle looking grey and broken.

When it was four years, everyone started frothing at the mouth and shouting swear words and how it was an injustice. It was, 'You're fucking joking, aren't yer?' and 'He deserves a fucking medal!' and so on, a big raging scrum with Ashleigh down at the front trying not to get buffeted. Aidan watched them all going deranged with anger, some of them with their eyes going in two directions, and said under his breath, 'Jesus,' and felt the prison officer tense up next to him.

He could have floored the fucker in one blow, vaulted the railing and been running down the street in fifteen seconds, but the prospect of four years in prison didn't bother him half so much as it seemed to bother his friends and relations in the public gallery.

After he had been led out, they all melted away and went to the pub. After a few pints they got more philosophical, and reckoned that although four years was a bit of a pisser, you probably couldn't go stabbing a man in the stomach twenty-seven times, even a paedo, and expect to be let off with a slapped wrist. And anyway there was something more urgent to deal with. Amy had been spotted lying down by the tramlines down at Castle Market, soliciting again.

'What did you bring Jay for?' Aidan said to Jasmine on the phone from prison.

'It's the nanny's day off,' she said, even though she was always leaving Jay on his tod. 'How is it?'

'It's exactly the same as remand. Anyway, I've only been here two hours. Plenty of time to get bum-raped yet.'

'For fuck's sake, Aidan,' she said. 'Be serious. I'm your mam. I'm allowed to ask if you're alright.'

'Aye, I'm fine,' he said.

And he was, because everyone had heard what a hard nut he was, and also what he had done to get in there, so he was treated like a hero. Everyone wanted to be bezzie mates, but Aidan just shrugged them off. He was perfectly friendly when people came up and talked to him, but he wouldn't join any gangs or owt like that. He mainly kept himself to himself.

'I don't want any trouble,' he said to one of the screws. 'I want to be out in a couple of years.'

The screw laughed. 'You? You'll paste some other poor fucker all over the walls and get time added on, not taken off. You want to get used to the food in here, because you're going to be eating it for a long time.'

23

AFTER AIDAN HAD been inside for three months, he heard from Ashleigh that Daniel from the car wash had got sent down too, six years for causing death by dangerous driving whilst pissed up and having a face which the judge didn't like.

That didn't mean fuck-all to Aidan.

Ashleigh visited Aidan every couple of weeks. They didn't have a lot to talk about, but that was alright. Aidan didn't talk a lot anyway, so Ashleigh jabbered on about any old shit and at the end of the session she would go quiet and they would try to say important things to each other. Aidan would say she looked really fit or ask if she was doing OK in the flat (she had moved out of her Uncle's Jim's after everything that had happened next door). Ashleigh would ask if Aidan was OK in prison and swear that she wasn't shagging anyone else. After she had gone Aidan would go back to his cell and have a wank, and while he was doing it it was the most exciting thing in the world, but afterwards he would lie on his bunk and feel sad. Tears would well up in his eyes and after a while his mind would turn to the house and the spare room and what had gone on there.

Then one time Jasmine came and said that Davey had been admitted to the hospital with a pain in his chest, and the doctors had run some tests and it was lung cancer.

After Aidan had been inside for about nine months,

Daniel got moved to the same prison because of some Eastern European gang stuff that he had got involved in in the last one. When he arrived he was the same loudmouth as before, telling everyone that Aidan wasn't such a hero as he seemed and boasting that Aidan's sister had turned tricks for him. People said that if Aidan didn't break his face then maybe there was some truth in it, but Aidan didn't lift so much as an eyebrow and went on doing gazillions of press-ups, looking at Marvel comics, and trying to make hooch in his cell.

Then one day they passed each other on the stairs. Daniel said, 'How much is your sister earning nowadays, Wilson? Twenty pounds a punter? That's all I gave her.'

'Shut your arse and give your mouth a chance,' said Aidan, and was going to move on past him.

'I heard you were a hard man. Seem pretty spineless to me.'

'It seems to me you're more interested in me than my sister,' said Aidan, 'so maybe I'll give you what you're asking for.' He threw his arm out and punched the sharp edge of his knuckle into Daniel's cheekbone, and when Daniel was falling on to the floor he stamped on his leg and broke his fibula and tibia.

All the prisoners said that Aidan had had no choice and was entirely innocent, but the prison authorities saw things in a different light. Aidan's offender supervisor said he could kiss goodbye to any thoughts of an early release.

'No shit, Sherlock,' said Aidan.

He got away with ABH, though, and that only meant an extra six months, instead of like ten years if he had been daft enough to stab the bugger.

After that things went a bit downhill. Aidan started whacking people round the back of the head with his dinner tray, or nutting them in the corridor if they looked at him funny. It was the usual hardman stuff, except Aidan didn't have to do it because everyone already thought he was this hero. Once he started belting people for no reason, they started to think that maybe he was just a tosspot after all.

Christopher Pugh, the white-collar fraudster he shared a cell with, lay in bed at night scared shitless while Aidan whimpered in his sleep in the bunk above. Then one morning there was a sour smell in the air, and although Christopher knew better than to spread it about that Aidan was a bed wetter, he thought that something ought to be done or one day he would wake up dead in his bed. So he had a word with the duty psychologist and the next thing, Aidan was hauled in to have a session with this shrink called Genevieve.

She asked him about how he felt and why he thought he did those things to the other prisoners, which she called destructive behaviour. When Aidan said, 'Dunno,' she said, 'Yes, but what do you *think?*' So he looked away into the corner of the room. But it was hard to ignore her because she was a woman and quite attractive too, even though she was a bit posh and probably, like, forty. An actual woman whose perfume you could smell. So after a while he got talking again.

They talked a bit about what had happened with Gary Lamb, and all about Aidan's relationships with family and friends and women and whether Davey had beaten him up when he was little and all that guff. It was boring to talk about and he let her know that, but every time he got the hump and tried to ignore her she just sat there, being an actual woman looking at him with an open expression on her face, and he got sucked into talking again.

He told her a lot of lies and some true things, and denied

things that were true and made up some stuff as well. At one point she said, 'Is this true, what you're telling me, or are you making it up?' and he shrugged and said, 'Some of it.' So then of course she was asking which bits and why did he make it up, was it to see her reaction, and did he want to impress her or shock her and did it make him feel good to feel that he had shocked or scared a woman. It took a long time to ask all this, pushing at questions carefully and leaving big gaps and letting Aidan decide what he was going to say.

He mainly said, 'Dunno,' but she pushed him and in the end he said what did it matter what he told her, he was in here and she was on the other side of the desk, at the end of the day she would go home and he'd still be here and he'd still have the dreams and she couldn't make them go away.

Then he noticed his face was wet and he wiped it with his hand and they had a rest and then started again, jabbing and sparring like two boxers, and Aidan was the one with the sick feeling because he had been told to throw the fight.

At the end of the session she told him he had post-traumatic stress disorder.

'Oh, right,' he said, in a what-a-load-of-bollocks kind of way.

'What do *you* think?' she said, again.

'I think I'm a stupid scrote who fucks everything up.'

'Why do you think that?'

'It's what the screws think.'

And so on. The next day he broke Christopher's nose for no reason at lights out, so there was clearly more work to do.

24

THE, WHAT GENEVIEVE called, 'violent incidents'
were adding extra days to Aidan's sentence willy-nilly. If
he kept it up he'd be looking at a fresh charge and next time it
might not just be a few months – it would be a few years, or
they would be carting him off to the loony wing.

Ashleigh had a face on when she came to visit.

'What are you getting time added on for? It's like you don't
want to get out and be with me. Am I supposed to just wait
around like a lemon?'

He told her about the cognitive behavioural therapy that
he had started with Genevieve. How she got him to tell her
everything about That Day, every second, what he had seen
and done, and how he had felt about it at the time and since.

'What do you want to go over what happened for?' said
Ashleigh. 'It's no good raking it all up again. And who the
fuck is Jennyviv?'

She was dead jealous, and it didn't help when Aidan said
Jennyviv was far too posh to look at the likes of him. 'Snotty
cow,' said Ashleigh, with steam coming out of her ears.

The trouble was, Ashleigh was only allowed two visits
every four weeks, and even that was difficult to manage. It
was a pig to move her shifts at Aldi, and also there was her
ice skating training.

She had always been good at skating, and now she had

started going to this club in Don Valley where they trained you up to be like Torville and Dean. She had been paired with this shopfitter called Marco, and they were training hard so they could enter some competitions. Everyone said they had potential. Of course Marco was boning her on the side. Maybe not then, but later, it happened. So all in all it was hard to find the time to visit Aidan, even though Ashleigh loved him and Marco was just this handsome jerk she skated with.

Whereas Jennyviv was there, waiting in the psychotherapy clinic, every Tuesday afternoon at two, wearing her relaxed trouser suit and smelling of Nicole Kidman. So it was no surprise, the more Ashleigh didn't turn up and the more Jennyviv sat there being nice to him, that Aidan developed a bit of a crush.

When Ashleigh did visit, it was Jennyviv this, and Jennyviv that, and maybe Ashleigh should talk to someone herself about what happened, to help her get over it.

'I am over it, actually,' she said.

When Aidan told her he was listening to these audiobooks, she made a face like he'd come out. Audiobooks weren't what she had signed up for. In fact, she hadn't signed up for anything. So what was she doing here?

Afterwards she wrote Aidan a letter saying she wasn't coming again because he was so selfish getting into fights and getting time added on, not thinking of her, and anyway she had her career to think about and maybe it would be better if they both just moved on, even though she was so grateful for what he had done and they would always have that between them, but also it did spoil it a bit to think that even if they got married and flew out to, say, Corfu for the honeymoon, there would be their memories of that house and what happened in it always in their heads between them.

She didn't mention Marco.

Aidan told Jennyviv and she said, 'I'm sorry to hear that.'

The audiobooks had only been for Aidan to have in his headphones when he was going to sleep at night, so that his brain had something to keep it busy. Then one day Jennyviv cocked her head on one side and said, 'Do you like listening to them?' like it was all part of a master plan to educate him and turn him into a rounded human being.

He said, 'No.'

But he did like the art book she leant him, the bright colours and that, by some guy called Keith Haring.

'You should go to the art classes,' said Jennyviv.

'Maybe,' said Aidan.

'It would look good,' she said. So he did.

At the class, he mainly did softporn pictures of punky girls on futuristic motorbikes, gothic cities and horrified faces swirling through the vortex of time. He did a few knife blades till another inmate leaned over and said that sort of thing didn't go down very well in here.

The teacher kept asking him to paint the bowl of fruit that was in front of him, but he never did, except this one time when he did the orange, apple and banana in really bright colours like the Haring bloke, and the teacher said it was very good, a real breakthrough. Aidan's eyes started to fill up, and then he snapped a paintbrush and walked out, and the next week it was back to the biker chicks smuggling peanuts in their leathers.

After the broken nose, Christopher Pugh had got moved to a different cell, and they put this loudmouth called Jake

in with Aidan instead. Everyone said Jake had backchatted
the screws one too many times and they had put him in with
Aidan as a punishment, hoping he'd lose his front teeth or
something. As it turned out, they got on like a house on fire,
running through lists of pop stars they'd like to shag and
comparing notes on house parties they had been to in South
and West Yorkshire, arguing about which estate was worse,
which drug was better. The destructive behaviour started to
taper off, and apart from the odd scuffle at the ping-pong table
Aidan got his head down, and the months went by.

25

B Y THE TIME Aidan got out of prison he was nearly twenty-two. The day he got out he went home to see Jasmine and she cooked him egg and chips. Davey was upstairs in bed looking like a zombie. He stank of sweat and illness. Aidan stood at the door and they looked at each other and nodded.

He said to Jasmine downstairs, 'I thought you were leaving him. After last time.'

'I couldn't, could I? With the cancer and that.'

She seemed to have forgiven Rikki too, because there she was popping in to drop off Jasmine's scratchcards.

'You've got a nerve,' said Aidan, but Rikki just laughed and helped herself to a bag of Monster Munch.

Jay was there, lying on the sofa watching *Top Gear* and scratching his knackers. 'Shouldn't you be at school?' said Aidan. Jay said it was the middle of August, and anyway when had Aidan ever cared about school? Aidan said, 'Jennyviv says . . .' and stopped.

All weekend Aidan was dropping hints about going up to Leeds to stay with Ryan, or maybe Wakefield with his mate Jake.

'You're not stopping here, then,' said Jasmine eventually.

'No.'

'Are you worried about seeing Ashleigh with this Marco? Aren't you going to try and get her back?' They lived up the hill in a right-to-buy, and Jasmine saw them all the time packing up Marco's Focus with skates and sequin dresses, and trolling off to competitions in Bradford and Gateshead and Bromsgrove and Coventry.

'It's been too long,' he said. 'Anyway, I've gone off her, and she's gone off me.'

But Jake from Wakefield had been rearrested for a different offence the day after he got out and was on remand, and Ryan had broken his ankle dirt-biking outside Preston, so it looked as if Aidan would have to stay on at his mum's. He signed on for Jobseeker's Allowance and spent his days knobbing around Castle Markets, trying his luck with parked cars and shoplifting on the Moor. Then he nicked this girl's mobile phone at the entrance to McDonald's. She shouted after him, 'Oi, give it back, you wanker,' and he turned round to give her some lip. They were standing on either side of the road trading insults for five minutes and it was basically like 'get a room'. Her mates gave each other a look.

Aidan sauntered back over the road and held the phone out. She grabbed it and cuffed him round the side of the head as hard as she could. 'You're a twat, you are,' she said. Her name was Madison and that afternoon she took him home to Park Hill flats with her and went to bed with him.

After that they were an item, and Madison liked marching round with her arm through Aidan's, showing him off and giving earache to all and sundry, hoping someone would give it back so Aidan would kick the shit out of them. Her two stony-faced mates from McDonald's had told her all about his big reputation and she totally loved it. She used to go about with a quarter bottle of vodka in her trouser pocket and get into arguments with people, and then ring up Aidan and ask him what he was going to do about it, bursting into tears and stuff to try to get him worked up.

'She's trouble, she is,' said Nick one afternoon in the beer garden of the Rutland Arms. 'She'll have you back inside. Or she'll get a bun in the oven. Imagine having her for a mum.'

'She's just a kid,' said Aidan. 'If she pisses me off too much I'll dump her.'

But Madison was dead into Aidan. 'When I first saw you,' she said, 'it was like a bomb had gone off in me knickers.'

It was weird having this reputation as a nutcase and your own seventeen-year-old girlfriend was madder than you were. Sometimes they'd see Ashleigh and Marco out and about. Once Madison discovered Ashleigh was Aidan's ex, she was dead keen to go to the same pubs, basically stalking her, trying to stoke up a reaction. It was like she was living in a soap opera. They used to sit a few tables away with Madison gobbing off, Marco looking pissed off and queasy, and Aidan and Ashleigh trying not to notice each other.

'How come?' said Madison when she found out Aidan had never slept with Ashleigh. 'Is she frigid or summat? Is she a born-again Christian?'

'I don't think so. I was inside the whole time we were together.'

'You were hardly together then, were you? Not like us.' And she grabbed his hand and put it on her tit.

But you could tell it bothered Madison, to think that Aidan and Ashleigh had this romantic connection even though they'd never done it. Like it was special, or something. 'I don't get it,' she said. 'Explain it to me,' as if Aidan had been unfaithful to her and she wanted to eat her heart out by hearing all the gory details. But Aidan just shrugged.

She started getting even more erratic, drinking vodka and orange like there was no tomorrow, turning all sorts of outrageous tricks in bed, and looking for more and more trouble. She scratched this girl's face in the queue for a club and then screamed blue murder at the bouncers when they wouldn't let her in. The bouncers looked uneasily at Aidan in case he kicked off but he just turned round and walked away down the pavement, and Madison followed him punching the back of his head and calling him all sorts of names.

'Jesus,' he said. 'What's the matter with you?' They put on a right show for the crowds of pissed people on West Street, abusing each other and her trying to smack him, him grabbing her hands, and then he got her into a taxi and she sobbed her eyes out, and when they got home they had sex twice and she told him she loved him, and then went to sleep or pretended to while Aidan lay on his back watching the window start to lighten, with a face like he wanted to kill himself.

They were still hanging around in Ashleigh and Marco's local. One day Ashleigh came over while Madison was in the bogs and Marco was at the bar.

'Why are you doing this?' she said, but Aidan just looked at her. Then Madison came back and saw Ashleigh standing there and all hell broke loose.

First a glass came flying along with some choice words, and then a table went over as she charged across the room. Ashleigh didn't take it lying down and she met Madison with a right to the chin. Next thing, they were rolling around pulling each other's hair and kicking out at each other, and Aidan was there trying to pull them apart. But Marco turned up and took the opportunity to kick this fucking ex of his girlfriend's in the face. The sharp edge of his poncy brogues caught Aidan flush in the cheek. It busted right open and a lot of blood came streaming out, and Aidan staggered back and only stopped when his arse hit the fruit machine.

Marco was standing there staring at him as if he was wondering what the hell he'd done.

Aidan had basically passed out and was only balancing there, so the men looked like they were probably done, but Ashleigh had Madison by the hair and was kicking her in the stomach, and Madison was wailing in pain and rage. Then Ashleigh let her go and she collapsed on the floor and chucked up, and everyone else who had been standing around in horror suddenly stepped forward and started trying to break it up now that the danger was over, like they always did.

Ashleigh and Marco gave each other this murderous glare and then Ashleigh walked out, and Marco followed her, but as he walked past Aidan he wagged his finger in Aidan's face and started to say something, but Aidan just reached out and grabbed his finger and wrenched it till Marco screamed, and as he ran out you could see that it was bent round like a question mark in completely the wrong direction.

26

AIDAN AND MADISON managed to wobble out of the pub before the police turned up, and it looked like no one made a complaint because nothing ever came of it, which was a good job because Aidan would have been straight back inside for a violation of the terms of his release.

Ashleigh said Marco had wanted to dob him in but she had told him if he did then it was over. They were meeting at this greasy spoon at Manor Top, and Aidan had been kind of hoping she would leave Marco and get back with him. But Ashleigh shook her head.

'Oh, Aidan,' she said. It seemed like getting into a brawl wasn't the best way to win back the love of your life.

'You ant dumped him, then? And he ant dumped you?'

She tossed her hair. 'He's right keen on me. He reckons we can win the regionals. But anyway, he still might have grassed on you except I said he might get charged as well. And he didn't want that.'

She was looking at Aidan with these sad but lovey eyes and it was totally obvious she still fancied him. But for some reason she resisted.

Aidan told Madison it was over. She was spitting tacks, laid up at her mum's with two black eyes, saying she was going to track Ashleigh down and stab her in the gut.

It was an odd thing to hear from a girl sitting on a bunk bed, surrounded by fluffy toys.

'Why?' said Aidan 'You're off your nut.'

'Hey, turn up the stereo and come here. We haven't done it since.'

'I don't think so. I've told you, we're no good together. Anyway, I haven't got any johnnies.'

'Oh fuck off, Captain Sensible,' said Madison.

Aidan left her sulking and pulling her hair into the tightest ponytail imaginable. Madison's mum caught him at the foot of the stairs.

'Here, have you trod dog shit into the carpet?' He hadn't, but that was her way of opening a conversation. The next thing, it was, 'You're nothing but an animal,' and, 'You've ruined our Madison's life.'

'Righto,' said Aidan. 'If she doesn't leave me alone, I'll ruin it proper.'

'What's that supposed to mean?'

It hadn't really meant anything, but quick as a flash Aidan said, 'I'll burn this fucking place down,' and this terrified look came over Madison's mum's face.

27

O F COURSE WORD got round about the fight in the pub, and everyone blamed Aidan. People sat round gossiping over a pint of Carling about Aidan being such a mad bastard.

Some said he had sold his soul to the devil, and some said he was like a pit bull and wanted his balls lopping off. Some said he was like a dog turd on a toddler's shoe. And they all agreed Aidan would be a good person to have an accident with a fork-lift.

Then Madison started a rumour that Aidan wasn't much to bother with, between the legs, and although that was just the sort of malicious shit that she would make up, it got confirmation from other sources. Another girl, who worked at the bookies, had taken him for a quickie in the back office, and she said that although he was good with his hands, the main event was a disappointment. 'Hardly worth using up my fag break for,' she said.

What with everyone saying what a bad human being he was, and Ashleigh still lying down with Marco for the sake of her skating career, living on the estate started to get Aidan down. He was drinking a lot and the dreams about Poppy and Gary Lamb were coming back worse than ever.

So he got on a train to Nottingham and went to visit Nick's mate Carl. Carl was living down there knocking out weed and pills and pirated DVDs. He had a kid by this girl Nina who lived round the corner and worked in a call centre and got silly at the weekends, pulling all-nighters and sitting up chewing the inside of her cheek and having the usual bullshit conversations about what was special about rave culture and how to bypass the gas meter and fractal videos and the CIA being responsible for JFK, saying, 'Fucking hell, mate,' a lot in her Nottingham accent.

Her and Carl were still shagging sometimes but they weren't in love or owt, so Carl lived in a shared house a couple of streets away and at the weekends he either took some gear round and joined the party or looked after Trixie for the night and didn't ask if Nina had slipped into bed with someone else.

At the moment he shared the house with Shelley Turner and Mark Crabbe, the psychos who had kicked the shit out of little Joe that time.

'What you hanging around with this pair of tosspots for?' said Aidan, after Carl had handed him a can.

'Nice to see you too,' said Shelley, giving him the rods.

'Leave it out, for fuck's sake,' said Carl. 'If you lot start brawling like morons you'll have the police down here in two seconds. And if they find my stash I'll say it's fucking yours.' He said that the three of them could only stay if they agreed to play nice, and they all said whatever, because they all needed somewhere to keep their heads down for a bit, and anyway Shelley and Mark were stoned and couldn't be arsed to move.

So the first night they sat about playing Tekken and smoking Carl's skunk, and that was like the pipe of peace. For a few weeks they all lived cooped up in the house, drinking a lot of white wine spritzers laced with vodka, because that was what they were into just then. Once a day one of them would go out for more supplies, and Aidan and Shelley and Mark took it in turns to run errands for Carl in return for smokes.

There was a steady stream of nervous students and lippy kids coming to score. Carl would sort them out and the others would totally ignore them.

'All these kids have got fucking knives,' said Shelley one day after a couple of strutting fourteen-year-olds had left.

'How do you know?' said Aidan.

'Cos she's a psychopath and she knows how their minds work,' said Mark, and Shelley put her hand in her jeans pocket and showed Aidan the top of a knife handle.

'Is that supposed to scare me?' said Aidan. 'All these kids have blades for the same reason. They're shit scared themselves.'

Just then Carl came back in from the toilet, so they shut up so as not to piss him off.

After that, whenever Carl wasn't there Shelley started going on about the knife, because she thought it shit Aidan up. She kept going on about what it felt like to stab someone and how it turned her on to walk down the street with her hand on it in her pocket, knowing what she was going to do with it.

'You're sick, you know that?' said Aidan, but she just laughed and kept going on about it all the more.

She started getting it out and telling him to look at it, trying to reflect the light from the window into his eyes, touching it all round her neck and even licking the side of the blade like it was Prince Charming's knob. Mark just sat there all the time laughing his piggy laugh. He was totally under her spell.

After a while Aidan put on his jacket and went out, just to get away from that pair of fruitloops. He'd promised Carl he wouldn't cause any trouble, and if he stayed there with them he was going to snap.

He started going in the snug of this old man's pub on the corner, sitting with the Nottingham Evening Post and a pint of mild and watching the sunlight move across the room. Sometimes people would talk to him and he would be friendly back without giving much away, and over the weeks he became a bit of a fixture.

There was a barmaid there who flirted with him. She was at least as old as his mum, but he went along with it and was thinking that at some point he might see if he could sleep with her. He was still thinking all the time at night about Poppy and Gary Lamb, and perhaps he thought that having a thing with an older woman would prove in his own mind that he wasn't like that himself.

She wore flimsy tops which showed all the flesh of her arms and the tanned and stretched and freckled softness of the top of her tits, and he used to stare at her and think, 'That's a woman and that's normal and I like it that way, and the only reason I think about the other stuff is because of what that dirty cunt did to Poppy, and that wasn't my fault.' And it was true that when he was awake in the middle of the night reliving the video that Gary Lamb made, he wasn't getting off on it at all. He was crying and feeling sick, and he would get out of bed and drink a glass of water and start to feel better. But then he would wake up the next night with the same dreams.

On a Saturday Carl took to calling in to the pub to watch the football results come in on the telly. He would park the pushchair by Aidan's table and buy Trixie a bag of crisps and a J2O, and he and Aidan would sit and talk about the old days on the estate, remembering all the stupid shit they used to get up to. Carl said that Aidan still hadn't learned and Aidan pointed at Trixie and said that he hadn't either.

One day Aidan said that those two psychos at Carl's place were driving him off his nut. He told him about the knife-licking and all the other mad-bastard hints they had made about killing people and getting off on it.

'I don't know why it bothers you,' said Carl. 'For them it's just fantasy. You've actually done it.'

'Keep your fucking voice down,' said Aidan. 'Anyway, I didn't enjoy it. It didn't get my rocks off like it does her. She's a straitjacket case. I don't know why you don't chuck her out.'

Carl looked embarrassed and mumbled something, and Aidan guessed that he was dipping his wick with her on the quiet. Or maybe not on the quiet. Mark was such a pathetic slave that he probably went along with it.

But Carl said he would have a word, and when Aidan went back later that night they were all sweetness and light, and the four of them swallowed a handful of pills each and listened to ear-bleeding techno till Carl said he had to go to sleep because it was starting to get light and Trixie would wake up in a couple of hours. Aidan went to bed as well.

When he woke up it was the middle of the day. There was no sign of Carl, and Aidan guessed he had taken Trixie round to her mum's house to cook Sunday lunch and hopefully get a sniff later.

Shelley and Mark were out as well, so he made himself a fried-egg sarnie and a mug of tea and settled down to watch some Formula 1, hoping to get his brain on an even keel.

The racing was boring as fuck and he started to drop off again. The next thing, the door had burst open and there was this dog licking his face and Shelley and Mark holding it on a lead and laughing their heads off. 'Here boy,' Mark kept saying, and Shelley said to Aidan, 'Ey up sadsack. We've brought you a bitch to keep you company.'

The dog was a mongrel that looked like it had spaniel and staffie in it. It was wagging its tail and still trying to lick Aidan's face. He was pushing it away and sitting up when suddenly Mark gave it a vicious kick in the side.

It yelped and flew across the room till it reached the end of the lead. Mark yanked the lead and the dog flew back towards him.

'What the fuck are you doing?' said Aidan and made to stand up, but Shelley leaned over the back of the sofa and held the knife to his neck. She started whispering these sick things about 'fucking his bitch' and 'showing him how to use a knife' that turned his stomach.

Mark kicked the dog again, and Shelley pushed the blade of the knife harder against Aidan's neck. He could feel that it was starting to cut into his skin, and he was aware of Shelley breathing harder and harder in his ear as if she was really getting a lob on.

Just then the door opened again and Carl walked in carrying a twenty-four pack of Carling.

'What the fuck's going on here?' he said.

'That's what I said,' said Aidan. The knife fell away from his neck, and now Shelley was shrugging and laughing.

'Just messing about, Carl, we're just having a laugh. No need to get your cock out about it.'

Mark gave the dog a last kick, but a half-arsed one this time, and dropped the lead. The dog shot under the coffee table and upset it.

'Jesus,' said Carl, and put the box of beer down on an easy chair. Aidan stood up and was working out which of them to hit first, but Carl put his arm out to stop him. 'Fucking leave it mate. They're fucking psychos. Get out,' he said to Shelley and Mark, 'and don't come back.'

Shelley stood there with a face like a smacked arse, but Mark was still laughing. They were as mad as each other. She said, 'It'd be a shame if someone tipped off the police about this place,' meaning Carl's dealing, but Carl just laughed and said, 'If you tell the teacher, I'll give you a Chinese burn.'

She was stood there simmering with rage. Aidan said, 'Earth to Planet Shelley: please vacate the galaxy,' and turned his back on her to coax the dog out from behind the telly.

Shelley whipped her knife out, but Carl picked up the coffee table and held it in front of him, saying, 'Back in your cage, Sheba. Put those teeth away.' The fact they weren't taking her seriously was making her mad as hell.

Mark was stood in the middle of the room trying to decide what to do. Aidan had the dog on a lead now and as he walked past he put his elbow in Mark's face and sent him sprawling, then left the room. He let the dog out the front door and came back down the hall, still grinning. 'I've killed one person in my life so far,' he said. 'It didn't make me spunk my pants like it would you, but I'd make it three without batting an eyelid. You might be able to scare little kids by treating a knife like an iced lolly, but to me it just means you belong in a mental home.' And he suddenly reached out and grabbed Shelley by the back of her hair, and Carl caught her arm and twisted it till she dropped the knife. Aidan dragged her up to the front door and chucked her out. Carl followed, marching Mark in front of him like a copper.

The two of them hung about shouting abuse in the street for a few minutes, and then went away. Aidan and Carl opened a can and congratulated each other on getting rid of them, but then Aidan said, 'They probably will grass on you, so if I were you I'd dump your stash round Nina's. And I think I'd better make myself scarce, too.'

So he packed up his bag while Carl nipped round to Nina's, and when Carl got back they drank another can for the road, and then Aidan set off again on his travels.

28

THERE WAS THIS lad Dave who had stayed at Carl's for a couple of nights while Aidan was there, and he and Aidan had got on pretty well. So Aidan gave him a call, and the next thing was he went over to Stockport to sleep on Dave's sofa in this beat-up old terrace. It wasn't a squat exactly because Dave was the legal tenant. He just hadn't paid any rent for a few months. He spent half his time at the Citizen's Advice, going over his rights with a fine-tooth comb, and he knew all the tricks: when to respond to a letter, when to ignore it, how to string the landlord along with promises and make it look cheaper to wait him out than to take him to court. 'It's a bit like keeping a girl on the boil,' he said. 'A bit of what they want to hear goes a long way.'

'I'll just sling my stuff down here, shall I?' said Aidan.

They went out for a stroll in the mornings, to see what they could see, and then hung around in the afternoons drinking and noshing dried mushrooms that Dave had collected last autumn. They would sit on the floorboards listening to old techno tapes and playing shithead, agreeing about how blown their minds were.

'It's like acid but less intense,' said Dave.

'And less boring,' said Aidan.

'Yeah,' said Dave. 'Less boring than acid.'

'Yeah.'

Then after like an hour of this Aidan would get up and go

and wash his face and open a can of cider, and the conversation would pick up again.

There was the usual crew of housemates stumbling about the place making out they were best buddies but keeping their bedroom doors locked and writing on all their food in permanent marker. There were half a dozen cartons of off milk in the fridge, but at least you could tell who they belonged to. They were all dolers and chancers like Dave and Aidan, except for this Chinese guy in the attic room who was doing an MA in International Relations at Manchester Met. He didn't know the rent was behind and he was paying for all the gas and electric on his tod.

'If he finds out we're fleecing him we'll have the triads on us,' said Dave.

'That's racist, that is,' said Aidan. But there was no chance of Bo Zhang finding out fuck-all, because he was always at college or playing squash or out meeting Chinese friends, and when he did come home he sprinted past the carnage downstairs and shut himself in his room to study. Dave said he ought to make more of an effort to integrate.

There was this group of folk that all used to turn up at the same parties in squats and student houses, empty polytunnels and warehouses. Lots of students of course and crusty traveller types and pillhead hard nuts who would take a spliff off you and split your lip if you said anything. It was a weird scene – like, up for it, with an edge. The hard nuts might have spoiled it except there was a large amount of ketamine going round, so if things looked like kicking off someone just broke the ket out and five minutes later it was like a dormitory in a scout hut. Dave and his mates were always in the thick of it, nipping up to Gorton for a bag of pills or setting up a sound system in the basement of a disused college building. After the party they would head off to Dave's house or somewhere else and make a night of it.

There was this girl called Suzie who had pink dreads and a pierced lip, a tattoo of an anarchist A on her shoulder and the kind of don't-give-a-toss attitude that made all the crusties swoon. Dave said she had, like, an aura.

'Yeah,' said Aidan. 'Plus, she's dead fit, int she?' And Dave didn't know what to say because that felt like it missed the point of what he was saying, and yet it was totally what he meant.

One night Dave got extra mashed and went off dancing till ten in the morning in the basement to some very interplanetary dub, and Aidan was left upstairs passing a bong round one way and a bottle of Jack Daniels round the other, nattering any old bollocks to Dave's mates, and this Suzie starts giving him the eye.

When the two of them had got cosy, but before they'd actually started getting off with each other, Aidan said, 'He's dead keen on you, Dave is, you know,' but Suzie looked away and said, 'Who?' and brushed some imaginary ash off her leg, so he figured there was no point being honourable.

They went up to bed and when they came downstairs again the ITN evening news was on and someone was making a big pan of veggie chilli. Dave was spragged out on the carpet draining cans of Foster's to make himself feel better. He was having trouble pointing both eyes in the same direction at once, but he waved them towards Aidan and Suzie and gave them a look like this kind of shit was exactly the comedown he was having. Suzie went through to the kitchen to get a bowl of chilli. Aidan sat down by Dave and Dave called him a cunt in a weary way, and Aidan grinned and passed him another Foster's and took one himself. He could smell Suzie on his fingers, and he smiled to himself again and then stood up and met her in the hall and took her back upstairs with the bowl of chilli.

The next day Aidan and Dave went out to play pool in the pub and Dave said it was fine about Suzie and he should just go for it, and Aidan said right, thanks, he would.

After that Aidan kind of got a bit obsessed with Suzie, and she kind of got a bit obsessed with him. It was like they got drunk off each other, and, since most days they really did get drunk and smoked a few spliffs and necked whatever was to hand, things got pretty full-on. They were the ones egging everyone on and shotgunning beer cans and disappearing upstairs with a bag of powder, telling each other to fuck off and die and telling everyone else to, smashing the window of Dixons, pegging it across flat roofs and down drainpipes, giving coppers the rods, throwing up and passing out with palpitations and having fits and generally giving the impression of Bonnie and Clyde going off the rails and sleepwalking towards the beckoning chasm of the grave.

One night there was a party out in a disused quarry outside Manchester and Aidan and Suzie wandered off with an air rifle, hunting rabbits in the dark. They blundered through the scrubland and came across an industrial estate. A security guy pointed a very powerful torch at them. He had a big barking dog at his side so they ran. They were completely disorientated. After a while they got to a chain-link fence so they vaulted over it and kept running, and the next thing they knew the ground had dropped away and they were falling down a bank of stones and cliffs and scree into the quarry. Everyone said Jesus Christ the stupid bastards could be dead and they should go to hospital, but they were already wired and they just drank a load more spirits, and it was only in the morning when the pain started to catch up with them. Aidan had sprained his ankle and bruised his arm and couldn't use it for weeks, not even to squeeze a sauce bottle, and Suzie had scraped away all the skin on the left side of her back and her hip and thigh.

Dave said what happened at the quarry was a warning and Aidan and Suzie needed to cool it down a bit.

Aidan said, 'Who are you, me mam?'

Then Dave started saying maybe Aidan and Suzie weren't good for each other. 'You're both my friends,' he said. 'I don't want to see either of you getting hurt.'

Aidan just said Dave was trying to split them up because he was jealous. 'You won't though. We're fucking solid. We're having a rare old time.'

'Christ,' said Dave. 'You've got it bad, you have. You're as bad as each other. You're a pair of lunatics.'

29

NOT LONG AFTER that Aidan had to nip back to Sheffy for a court appearance, and since Nick was at a loose end they met up and made a weekend of it. There was an England game on the Saturday night so Aidan walked through town waving an Argentina flag shouting 'Malvinas!' But since England were playing Albania and hardly anyone knew what Malvinas meant, he got nothing out of it but a few funny looks, and Nick told him to stop being such a twat.

'What's the matter with you?' he said. 'You've never been this bad.'

'Oh, it's this bird,' said Aidan. 'She's sent me off me nut.'

He peeled the label off his beer bottle and stared at it as if he was about to open up, but then Nick started going on about all this grief he was getting from having it off with some girl, and how he hated those Polish cunts, and so on, so Aidan just switched off.

When he got back to Stockport and asked where Suzie was, everyone gave him these knowing looks and then found somewhere they needed to be in a hurry. It was obvious that something had gone on. He set off round the usual pubs and found her in a beer garden, pissed out her head and draped over some bastard with a crew cut and a signet ring.

'Where the fuck have you been?' she shouted at Aidan and chucked a pint glass at him, and she kept on raving away till Aidan was about to fuck off and leave her to it. The crew cut and his mates were all pissing themselves, partly at Aidan and partly at her, and then one of them pulled out a phone and started playing a video of Suzie pissed and in the buff, letting two or three of them shag her any which way, all at the same time. They were laughing their heads off in the video and in real life and so was Suzie, except her laughter was kind of hysterical, like what the fuck is going on in my life, and the couple at the next table were standing up and leaving without finishing their drinks as if to say, these new smartphones are really something but maybe they need tighter regulation and we don't feel safe here, and thank Christ there aren't any children present. The crew cut was laughing in Aidan's face, but although Aidan's fists were clenched white and his face was pure bad news, he just turned and walked off and left them to it.

Suzie turned up again stony-faced on the Thursday, looking half sorry as hell and half don't you dare mention what happened if you want me to stay.

So at first Aidan didn't say anything and they drank vodka all afternoon and ended up in bed together, and after it had all calmed down and they were all lovey-dovey again he said, 'What the fuck was all that about?'

Of course she spouted off then, having a go at him and calling him all sorts of names, but he let it pass off and then kept asking, all nice like, and plying her with cans of ale, and over the next couple of days he started to wheedle the story out of her.

It wasn't much of a story though – something about her shit life back in Swansea growing up and being bashed around by her dad and worse shit by her dad's friend. At that Aidan sank into a black mood, and then he told her about Poppy, which she sort of knew about already, but he tried to tell her some of the details. But she snapped at him to shut up, swivelled her legs out of bed and started to pull her knickers on and then her leggings. She said she didn't want to know.

'Jennyviv says . . .' said Aidan, but she said, 'Who the fuck is Jennyviv?' and as always it was hard to argue with that. But after that conversation he was a lot more careful about having a mad bastard for a girlfriend, and even though they'd hardly told each other fuck-all it was like they were closer now. Less innocent, mind – sort of a proper couple but also like they were really enemies waiting for the next war to break out.

When they were sober one or other of them would start getting these morbid thoughts and mulling things over in what Jennyviv would have called a really unhealthy way, and the next moment they'd be turning the air blue and threatening each other with garden shears.

By far the safest way to live was to get drunk as early in the day as possible and then keep topping up the booze and partying until it was time to go to sleep again. A bit of scraped skin every now and then was better than a full-on breakdown. There was always the likelihood of all that booze rotting your internal organs, but that was something to worry about later. Aidan said, 'Jennyviv says if you make enough noise you can almost drown out your true feelings,' and Suzie said, 'Sounds good to me.'

'What if you get pregnant?' said Suzie's friend Bron. 'You're not telling me he uses a condom when you're both out of your skulls.'

Suzie just laughed. 'Half the time he's good for nothing. And even when he is – his sperm's not winning any swimming races.' Bron had watched this documentary about the effects of alcohol and other recreational drugs on growing foetuses, but she just pursed her lips.

Eventually the landlord got in to effect the eviction order on Dave's house, and changed the locks. They all got back from an all-nighter down in Congleton to find their stuff in a skip and a couple of thugs stood by the front door looking ready for anything.

Dave got up in the skip and started rooting around and loading the stuff that was worth it into the back of his Punto. He said he would go and stop at his mum's but there wasn't any room for the rest of them. Aidan and Suzie said goodbye and walked down the street, and round the corner Suzie said, 'That's it then,' and they had a blazing row in broad daylight on a Sunday morning without either of them knowing what it was about.

In the end Suzie said she was going back to Swansea and Aidan said he'd come too. She said, 'Fine.' They got on a train and drank some Strongbow on the way, but it all felt wrong.

When they arrived at Suzie's old estate she said, 'Jesus Christ, back here again,' and burst into tears. Then she sat on a swing in the playpark weeping while Aidan went to the Spar for a bottle of brandy and a few cans.

30

S UZIE'S MUM WAS dead but her stepdad Steve still showed an interest, as if she was his real daughter. He said she and Aidan could have the spare room, which pissed Billy her stepbrother off because that's where he had been keeping his gym equipment.

'Nicked, is it?' said Suzie, and he scowled.

'Alright, mate?' said Aidan, but Billy blanked him.

Suzie's stepdad had trouble with his mobility. There was a ramp up to the front door but the funding had run out before the council had fitted a stairlift, so most of the time Steve slept on a mattress in the lounge, unless Billy or Suzie or Aidan happened to be there to help him upstairs. The trouble was, if there was no one else in the next morning then he was stuck up there with no breakfast and no way of getting down. He kept a multipack of crisps by the side of his bed for emergencies, and there was a wall-mounted flatscreen up in the corner by the pelmet. There was dust that thick – no one had cleaned the place since Suzie's mum died, and Steve couldn't have reached that high even if he'd wanted to. He just lay on the bed with his memories and crossed his fingers there wasn't a fire.

'Don't you get a wheelchair?' said Aidan.

'Not till I've been reassessed. The last numpty said I could manage with sticks.'

They were holding off on the reassessment because Steve

was due to go in for a procedure that the doctors were hoping might make him more mobile again. And obviously there was no point spending money on a problem that might go away in the mean time. Till then, Steve would have to grin and bear it. The waiting list was eight months.

But Steve didn't let it get him down. Partly it was just that he had a sunny disposition, and partly it was because he was on these monster painkillers. Billy kept on at Aidan not to let Suzie near them. 'They're opiates,' he said. 'Once she gets a handful of them down her neck she'll be back on the smack in no time.'

'Oh, right,' said Aidan like that was no surprise, although Suzie had never mentioned having been a smackhead. Suddenly the lost weekend with that crew cut cunt started to make sense.

He said, 'Our Amy's done her time on the gear.'

Billy said, 'I don't give a fuck about your Amy. Just make sure Suzie stays off it.'

But Billy was pissing in the wind, because once Suzie had been back in town for a week or so, she bumped into some of the no-marks she used to knock about with. Even though most of them weren't using at the time, there was plenty of methadone sloshing around, and soon enough Suzie was trying the odd medicinal tot. And from there it was a matter of time before she was smoking a bit of brown and telling Aidan it was no big deal, not like sticking a needle in your arm.

Aidan thought about Steve's tablets and Billy's angry face and his nightmares about Poppy wotsit and Suzie's slack-faced bliss, and five minutes later he was having a puff himself. They had a lovely afternoon at this bloke Dennis's damp flat and then went home, picking up a three-litre bottle of cider on the way.

When they got back, the house was empty. There was a note from Steve saying there had been a cancellation and he had gone to hospital to have his procedure early, and he would be in for a week and would they bring him a few clean t-shirts and some Lucozade? Billy was up in Liverpool on a labouring contract, and as Aidan was tugging off Suzie's jeans he thought what a fucking brilliant summer it was going to be.

They spent that week getting out of it in the house, with all Suzie's old mates coming round with a little something to help pass the time. They said it was like the old days, and the way they went on it sounded like Swansea a few years before had been sunnier than Ibiza and madder than the Haçienda. Aidan got along very well with everybody. He always had a smile on his face, and they said you could see he was good for Suzie, just look at her. She was up the whole time, nattering on and mouthing off, dancing and sitting down and getting up and giving the room the rods with a big smile and shouting fuck off with a glint in her eye. Things were getting very messy but it was okay, because on the Friday Steve was going to get discharged, so the day before they would get a grip of themselves and tidy up the house or at least bag up the empty cans and put fresh water in the bong, and after that everything would get back on more of an even keel.

Then on the Wednesday Suzie got a call from Billy who said the hospital had phoned to say Steve had had some complications and maybe someone could go in to visit, and Billy said why the hell hadn't they been to see him and why hadn't they been answering the landline?

'Never heard it, mush,' said Suzie. 'It's not part of my soundtrack. What do you mean, complications?'

Complications meant some bad shit, maybe septicaemia maybe not, maybe a reaction to the drugs, but anyway Steve was in a bad way and Billy was going to get tomorrow off or the day after but in the mean time Suzie had better get down the hospital soon. 'Like now. This afternoon. He might die.' There was an accusation in his voice that meant, yeah, now the difference between a son and a stepdaughter was becoming clear.

'Alright,' she said. 'I'll get straight down there.'

She got off the phone and told Aidan what had gone on. It was a real headfuck, and they had a spliff to calm down and then Aidan asked her if she was going to see Steve like she said to Billy. 'Yeah,' she said, 'but not today. I can't get my head round it, like. I'm too mashed. I'll have a night off and go in and see him first thing tomorrow when I can think straight.' Since there was no rush they skinned up again and opened a can of lager each to wash it down.

That was the night Suzie used a needle again, with her old mates Dennis and Bethan sitting on either side and a bit of very dark house pumping away on Steve's old Pioneer that had a wooden case but still sounded sweet as fuck. Aidan didn't want to stick a needle in his arm and the others called him a pussy in a jokey way, but he sat with them and had a good time anyway with a bottle of gin and some bitter lemon and a few smooth pills, and the next day they carried on where they left off, and suddenly it was a full week later and Suzie was mad as shit at Aidan for not making her go to see Steve and not stopping her getting back on the smack. She belted him and split his lip and smashed the kitchen window, and

Dennis and Bethan melted away but came back later tapping at the back door with some Jose Cuervo they had nicked from the Oddbins up in town.

So it went on. Going to see Steve, who probably stank of illness, before he died was this terrible chore hanging over them, but they tried not to think about it, and somehow the whole summer slipped by. Every couple of days Billy was on the phone mad as hell at Suzie for not visiting and finally when she said, 'Where the fuck are you? He's *your* dad,' it came out that he had got into a fight outside a club in Southport and now he was on remand for wounding with intent, so he wasn't coming back to Swansea any time soon. So he couldn't say shit.

31

THEY FINALLY GOT it together to go to the hospital, and there was Steve all wizened in bed like the living dead, which by the looks on the nurses' faces was exactly what he was.

'They've had to amputate me leg,' he said, and you could tell from the way the sheets sat that it was true.

Aidan and Suzie stared at the gap with open mouths like this was the worst day out ever. Suzie said, all choked up, how sorry she was for not visiting, and shooting Aidan an evil look as if it was his fault, but Steve waved it away. 'It's alright,' he said. 'You've been busy.'

Afterwards Suzie threw up into a bin and they went to the park where she sobbed and called Aidan a fucking bastard and then begged him to get some cash to buy some gear. He refused and she said again what a bastard he was, and told him to bog off back to Sheffield. So he marched off to the bus station.

Waiting for a bus he drank a couple of cans, and then picked up a brick and went into a newsagents and made them empty the till. He thought Suzie would be long gone from the park and anyway time was of the essence so he pegged it.

Back at the estate he called in at Bethan's and asked her to put him in touch with her dealer. A sly look came over her face. 'Only if you fuck me,' she said, so he did, and afterwards she took him over to the guy's place on Geiriol Road, and he bought some gear and took it back to the house for Suzie. Of course she was all smiles then. They made up and things went on as they had before.

Weeks passed. Steve was doing his best to fight off the infection but he wasn't in any state to come home, Billy was waiting for his court date, and Suzie and Aidan were drinking, fighting, scoring, using, breaking and entering, fucking, blaming anything and everything on each other and themselves, and generally sinking into the depths of despair.

Then one night sitting around a bucket, Bethan told Aidan cool as you like that he better get himself tested for hepatitis B, and Suzie went fucking ape.

First she belted Aidan over the head with one of Billy's dumbbells, and while he was there on his hands and knees trying not to pass out, with blood running down his face and collecting at the end of his nose, she headed off to the kitchen to look for a knife to finish the job. When Bethan tried to stop her Suzie grabbed her by the hair and swung her round so hard that a clump came out. She was whacking Bethan's head against the door frame when Aidan came up behind her and picked her up and held her while she struggled till she ran out of steam.

Every time he let her go she ran at him again and he had to hold her by the wrists to protect himself. She was spitting in his face and trying to kick him in the bollocks, and Bethan was there saying, 'Leave her, the crazy bitch,' and Suzie was going, 'Yeah, fuck off with your little tart,' and in the end Aidan did have to leave because there didn't seem any other way of stopping it. And since he had nowhere else to stay he did go back to Bethan's with her, and went to bed with her again, only this time he made her break into her little brother's room to borrow a condom.

So then Aidan was staying at Bethan's house but sneaking over to Suzie's every day to try to talk to her and make sure she was OK. She wouldn't talk to him and most days he just sat on the kerb outside while she sat around drinking inside, or if she didn't seem to be in he walked the streets looking for her. He remembered about the crew cut dicks in Stockport and figured things could get a whole lot worse now, with the state Suzie was in. He was drinking a lot himself and when Bethan wasn't off her face or seeing out her community service they were either shagging or fighting about shagging. Some days that Dennis would turn up with a bottle of Netto whisky and he and Aidan would get drunk till Bethan threw a wobbly or draped herself over Dennis's lap, and either way Dennis cleared off pretty sharpish. And sometimes Suzie would get mellow drunk and let Aidan in and they'd sleep together and Suzie would weep and then they'd start fighting again, and other times strange men would leave the house and smirk at him and then Suzie would leave as well, ignoring him, and Aidan knew she was heading over to the house on Geiriol Road.

By now it was winter, filthy weather, and Bethan's little brother was showing Aidan how he had sharpened an ornamental throwing star so that it wasn't ornamental any more, and her mum was cooking him fish fingers and calling him a nasty piece of work all in the same breath. It was all getting bleak as fuck. Bethan said, 'We could have a baby, you and me,' but Aidan turned to face the woodchip. Bethan lay there seething and then dug her nails in his back and said she'd kill him and Suzie too, so he turned back to face her just to calm her down.

The next week Bethan told him that she'd heard that Steve had died, so he headed over to Suzie's and shouted up to the bathroom window that he was sorry to hear what had happened, he'd thought Steve was an alright fella and he was sorry he was dead. But after a very long silence Suzie shouted back that he was an evil devil trying to fuck with her mind, and she never wanted to see him again, so he went home. Then Bethan admitted she had made it up about Steve dying to see what he would do, and he grabbed her arm and banged it down on the edge of the fridge, and even though he didn't do it all that hard, it broke her wrist.

He walked her down to the hospital and waited in A&E while she got seen. He didn't know what she told them, but although the police were there to see about this kid who had got stabbed, nobody said anything to him.

'We're even,' said Bethan on the bus home, not looking at him, and after that Aidan slept on the sofa, but she didn't chuck him out even though her mum said what was the point having a gorilla about the place if you weren't getting any gorilla bone. It was pretty obvious that Bethan was biding her time till things had blown over so that she could get back with Aidan.

Aidan gave Suzie a few days after what had happened, and then he went over to say sorry. But when he got there, there was an ambulance and a police car outside and paramedics traipsing in and out. Billy was there, fresh from the train from Liverpool where he had finally got let off on time served. He went at Aidan like a lunatic, effing and blinding, and had to be restrained by a couple of policemen. It turned out that he had arrived home to find Suzie slumped with a TV flex around her neck, under the banisters. It was only because she had done such a half-arsed job and the hall floor was taking most of her weight that she wasn't dead, and even so it was touch and go whether she could be revived.

At the hospital the doctors were all serious and uneasy. Even if she did wake up it was the kind of coma that gave you brain damage. It all depended how long she had been there before Billy found her. All they could do was wait and see. And so on. Billy was beside himself. He went out into the waiting area and lamped Aidan and knocked his front tooth out, and when Aidan was on the floor he just stood there kicking him and kicking him until security managed to haul him away.

'If I ever see you again I'll kill you,' he said.

Aidan said, 'I don't blame you.'

He walked back to Bethan's to pick up his stuff and on the way he thought about jumping in front of a bus himself, but that seemed like a bit of a me-me-me thing to do, so instead he broke into a house and took a bit of cash and a smartphone, and then hopped on a train back to Sheffy.

32

WHILE ALL THIS was going on, Davey was in a bad way. He had refused another round of chemo, and now he was in a hospice. Jasmine and Jay visited him every day, and Nick popped in a couple of times in the week. At the weekend they went in force: Jasmine and Jay and Nick, Kayla (but not Steven), and Martin (but not Amy).

They stood round the bed and stared at him, went off for a pee, pulled up a chair, coughed, read the paper, and tried to think of things to say.

'Where's Aidan?' said Davey, and Nick said, 'Who knows?'

Jasmine said he had dropped off the grid, and if you rang him up you got number not recognised. 'We don't know he's in any trouble,' she said.

'It'll catch him up soon enough,' said Davey. 'It follows him round like the CSA. Poor sod. Leave him out of it. I mean the funeral. I don't want fisticuffs at my wake.'

Then Amy turned up after all, shouty-weepy and remorseful, either pissed or grief-stricken or both.

'You're a disgrace,' says Martin, but she goes, 'Keep your tits on. He's *my* dad.' And they let her have a few minutes with Davey on her own, holding on to his hand and whispering to him and crying.

'She'll be saying how sorry she is,' said Jasmine, 'and promising she'll get better, like she always does.'

The next day he died. They still couldn't get hold of Aidan, so Davey got his wish. It was a good funeral, boozy but well-behaved. Amy was on the pineapple juice. All the family, bar Aidan, were there, and plenty of folk off the estate who Davey had used to deal to or have round for barbecues. There was only one full row of empty seats. Not bad for a grumpy old prick, as Nick said to Jay. Jay, who was fifteen by this time, was a bit red around the eyes. Davey's coffin went in to the Roses' 'I Am the Resurrection', which wouldn't have been allowed in church but at the crematorium they didn't give a toss. It was Davey's idea of a joke.

Davey's death came at a funny time for Nick. He was a bit stalled at work. The money was good, but not that good, and it seemed like he couldn't go any further without a degree or the right breaks, and he couldn't be arsed with one and the other didn't seem to come along. He worked hard during the week, and at the weekends he partied just as hard, getting through a serious amount of coke. Sometimes he said if he had a more interesting job he wouldn't need to go so wild on his days off, and sometimes he said he wanted to jack in having a job at all so he would have more time for getting trolleyed.

Either way, he had been caning it for a while, and then his dad died. He got a few days compassionate leave, and topped it up to a couple of weeks with his unused holiday.

Of course there was arranging the funeral, but once that was over he just sat around at Jasmine's house, watching a bit of telly, helping his mum go through Davey's stuff, putting plenty of Foster's away and playing GTA3. He said he was there to make sure Jasmine was okay, but really, Davey had been ill so long that him dying was a relief for her. Having

Nick in the house, another man to clean up after, was neither here nor there.

The first few days, he kept a bit of a lid on things. At the funeral he drank lager and then scotch, and only in the small hours sitting around deep in reminiscence with Jasmine and Kayla and Jay did the weed come out and get passed round in Davey's memory. But on the Saturday Connor turned up with some MDMA powder, and that was the start of a three-day bender.

'You're turning into your dad already,' said Jasmine on the Tuesday. 'Sitting in his chair, plotting your next dodge. Don't forget you've got a job to go back to. A proper job. Like he never had.'

But of course he did forget. Living back at home again, stewing over Davey's death, drinking in the afternoon with Connor and Carl, who was back from Nottingham, it was like he'd gone back to being a teenager again. He was worse than Jay. At least Jay went off to college every day, and had a girlfriend who was planning to go to university.

On the next Monday morning Nick was out of the house, and though Jasmine hoped he had gone to work she knew he would be hungover at Connor's or somewhere. He didn't come back that night, or the next morning, so the next time Jasmine saw him was the Tuesday evening, when he'd already missed two days of work. Even that would have been okay. He could have squared it with the company by playing the dead dad card and throwing himself on their mercy. But he said it was too late and refused to look her in the eye, staring grimly at *Deal or No Deal* on the telly. The next day he slept in till lunchtime, and then went straight out for breakfast in town, and before long it was the end of the week and he'd got his P45.

After a few weeks he had a problem. He was still guzzling down the vitamins, but there was no money coming in to pay for them. Connor was doing a bit of dealing on the side. It was Connor who was providing most of the stuff Nick was guzzling. So Nick, who had a bit more ambition than Connor, went in with him, and within a few months he was dishing it out on three estates and making more than he ever did at the works.

33

J ORDAN SMITH'S SISTER Teagan was still going out with Karol from the car wash. Karol and Nick used to see each other about, and there was always an air of aggro, but they never did anything about it. Karol had never paid Nick back for the brick through the windscreen, and they all knew about Aidan giving little Daniel what for in prison.

Jordan Smith was still sulking over how Aidan had kicked him up the arse. One night he was drinking a can of Kronenbourg outside the kebab shop, waiting for his 8-inch Americano, when Nick pulled up in his Subaru. Jordan stood on the bench and started shouting all sorts of bollocks, fucking this and what's your chuffing that you cunt. Nick tried to walk past and ignore him, but Jordan jumped down off the bench and got right in his face. Jordan was bladdered and Nick was sober and six inches taller, so there was no mystery about what would happen.

'I just want a chiliburger mate,' Nick was saying, and trying to push past, but Jordan was dancing around like a boxer getting in his way, calling him the usual string of things that people call each other when they're het up.

In the end Nick gave him a firm little shove, which sent him off balance. He might have gone over except the litter bin was in the way. He sort of sprawled backwards on top of it and then used it as a springboard to come and take a swing at Nick. But Nick was standing waiting for it and just moved out of the way, tipping Jordan over as he went past, so that he ended up on his hands and knees on the pavement, groggy.

'Now get up and fuck off,' said Nick, 'or I'll have to give you a kicking.'

It wasn't clear whether Nick knew this or not, but Jordan's sister Teagan was leaning in the doorway of the kebab shop watching. She came out now and they looked each other in the face as she walked past. 'Sorry,' she said, 'thanks,' and smiled. Nick stood and watched as she helped Jordan get up and gave him a quiet bollocking, and took him off towards the estate. She looked back over her shoulder at him watching.

The next thing, Nick and Teagan were at it on the quiet. Nick would prowl round in his Subaru and pick her up on the corner by the hot pork sandwich shop.

'Like a prozzie,' he said.

'Fuck off,' she said, but she was grinning.

They would drive out to somewhere posh like the Strines Inn or Fox House, park the car and then go for a walk, lie down and shag in the heather. Afterwards they would go back to the pub and have a meal, Teagan giggling and pulling stray bilberries out of her cleavage.

She told Lisa it was all so Polish with Karol, eighties soft rock ballads and conversations about history, and she didn't like the way he'd started wanting her to cook for him. With Nick it was a dab of coke and a white wine spritzer, and his hand up her skirt under the table. A real thrill, like it had hadn't been with Karol for she didn't know how long.

Lisa always thought Nick was a bit square, but Teagan said he had really loosened up.

He was so loosened up that he got sloppy about condoms,

and Teagan, who was totally into the naughtiness of it all, didn't say owt. But then her period was late and it completely shit her up because Karol, who already had a daughter he never saw from when he was back in Poland, had had a vasectomy. She sat in the Subaru, parked up at the bus stop outside Fox House, and sobbed. Nick looked pissed off but he tried to comfort her.

He said at least they had caught it early, but Teagan said she didn't even know if that's what she wanted to do She didn't think she was ready but part of her really wanted it, and she didn't want to hurt Karol, and she had to think about who she really loved and who loved *her*, and what would be best for the baby or maybe that was just the hormones talking and she should just get rid of it. It was all whirling round in her head and would it be alright if they just sat and cuddled each other this time?

Nick yes it was fine, but in a way that meant no it totally wasn't. So when they drove out and parked up by a log pile at the edge of a conifer plantation, she leant over the handbrake and put her head in his lap.

It was awkward afterwards, and maybe because of that he took her straight home, instead of to the pub. Usually she had a chance to clean herself up in the pub toilets. When she walked in she knew she looked untidy, and anyway she was all flustered from going over everything in her head, and Karol looked at her strangely and she started to get a really bad feeling.

It turned out that Sebastian had seen her getting into Nick's car that morning. When Karol confronted her she was still sconned out with being late and what had happened with Nick at the plantation, and instead of twisting him round her little finger like she usually did, she blurted it all out and said that she was pregnant and Nick was the father and she didn't know if she loved him, and she loved Karol for definite but she didn't know if she loved Nick more or didn't love him at all. At first it seemed like Karol was going to hit her, but he didn't, he just shouted a lot and wagged his finger in her face, then chucked her out in the street and threw a handful of leggings and knickers and so on after her and shouted, 'Bitch,' and slammed the door. So she went round to her mum's.

That night she came on, so if she had just kept her mouth shut, everything would have been fine. But the genie was out of the bottle.

Karol turned up looking for Nick, shouting and hammering on the door. So Jasmine opened it and told him Nick wasn't there.

'I don't believe you. You're a fucking liar.'

'Don't speak to me like that. I'll scratch your eyes out,' she said, and they stood glaring at each other, and suddenly they both had the same idea, even though Jasmine was fifteen years older than he was.

The next minute they'd gone inside and shut the door, and Sebastian had to sit in the car playing Puzzle Bobble on his phone.

'Only if you promise not to go after Nick,' she said, as they manhandled each other in the hall.

'Promise.' They were proper snogging and tugging at each other's clothes, like a promise made like that would mean fuck-all.

It barely took ten minutes, but Jasmine told him afterwards it was the best sex she'd ever had. She knew he was the last person she should be saying that to, but there was no one else.

'It's because we were both angry,' he said, 'and didn't your husband die? Is how you get over your grief.'

He was playing with her hair. They were both smoking cigarettes.

'Are you angry now?'

He smiled, more to himself than to her. 'No.'

34

KAROL KEPT HIS promise, sort of. He didn't come for Nick with a baseball bat like he'd meant to. But he made sure it got round that he had slept with Nick's mother. When Nick got to hear about it, he asked Jasmine, and she laughed it off and said it was a load of bollocks. Nick said to Teagan that this showed Karol wasn't going to do anything, he was just making up stupid rumours.

They were together now, officially, although Teagan was still at her mum's, and it didn't seem as exciting as when they were sneaking off to the Peak District. Teagan didn't see as much of Nick as she would have liked, and when she said, 'What *would* you have done, if I'd been pregnant?' he said, 'But you're not.' Teagan's mum wanted to know what Nick did all day, and was he looking for a job? Of course Nick was knocking out quarters and eighths and handfuls of wraps, and the last place he was thinking of going was the job centre. But you couldn't tell Teagan's mum that. She was dead straight.

Then one Saturday they bumped into Karol and Sebastian in the beer garden of The Duke of Cumberland. They were pissed, the lot of them, and that was why it all kicked off.

Karol leaned over and said, 'Your mother said I was the best she ever had. The first since your father.'

'Let's go,' said Teagan, pulling on Nick's sleeve, but he wouldn't.

'You what?' he said.

'I bet the neighbours heard us. She was really screaming. Shaking all over and kissing me, like this - and this.' He pursed his lips and dotted dainty kisses over his own arms. 'And then she bit me. Here.' He pulled down his t-shirt to show the remains of what could have been a lovebite but maybe was just a bruise from walking into some scaffolding drunk.

Nick went for him then, but Sebastian was too quick and sent him flying with a punch to the chest. Nick sat on the floor, winded, and Karol and Sebastian stood up laughing and walked out.

He stormed out the pub after them and Teagan followed, trying to stop him. But he wasn't going after Karol. He got in the Subaru, so she jumped in the passenger side, and he drove off, fast, towards home.

At home he ran up the path, opened the door and slammed it before Teagan had a chance to follow. She waited, feeling sick, out the front, listening to the shouting inside. Then the door opened and Nick burst out again, grabbed her arm and pulled her along with him back to the car. She looked back and saw Jasmine coming out through the open doorway in her vest and socks, crying and shouting, but Nick pulled away with a roar before she got to the car.

He drove so fast that Teagan wet her knickers for fear of what was going to happen. He took them all the way down the Prince of Wales Road without taking his foot off the floor, weaving in and out of the traffic, running three red lights. Straight over the roundabout and then round in a horrible curve, losing the car's back end, on to the Parkway. Halfway to the M1, he lost it trying to undertake a Tarmac lorry, bounced off the barrier and slid sideways at speed into the concrete pillars of a bridge.

Nick was mashed up into little bits. It was one of the worst the emergency services had ever seen, a case of vomiting on the hard shoulder and taking the rest of the day off.

Teagan got lucky. She was badly hurt, but she lived. She had to have a piece of bone removed from her leg, and ever afterwards she walked with a limp. She had anxiety problems too, from what it was like in the car while she was waiting for them to cut her out. But she used the months when she was in hospital to have another stab at her GCSEs, and eventually she got on a course to study midwifery in Bradford, and afterwards she got a job at a hospital on the Wirral, and she never lived in South Yorkshire again.

Karol wanted to visit her while she was in hospital, but while she was unconscious her mum wouldn't let anyone, either him or anyone from Nick's family, in to see her. After she was on the mend and able to decide for herself, she asked for Jasmine, who would come and sit on the bed and talk to her as if they had been proper in-laws, even though while Nick was alive they had hardly spoken to each other.

But Teagan wouldn't see Karol at all. She said the problem wasn't Karol and Jasmine shagging each other. It was a free country. But what had killed Nick was Karol rubbing it in his face that he had shagged his mum. 'And it's, like, disrespect to you, isn't it, like he only shagged you to get at Nick.'

Jasmine said, 'Yeah,' and blushed.

So that was why Teagan blamed Karol and wouldn't see him after Nick died. At first he would turn up at the hospital and ask to see her, and then get angry when he wasn't allowed. But after that had happened a few times, he stopped coming and started laughing about the whole thing instead, going around saying Nick's temper had been the death of him, and

Teagan wouldn't be so flexible in bed now that she was a cripple, that it was usual to burn the body before scattering the ashes, and so on and forth. His cronies laughed and he generally put it about that he was glad that things had turned out as they had.

35

ONE DAY A few months later, Aidan walked in the door and made himself a cheese sandwich.

'And where the fuck have you been?' said Jasmine.

Aidan said that he had been shacked up with this girl in Swansea, taking a lot of drugs and losing it. But now he was back.

Jasmine told him that his dad and his brother were both dead. He sat down and rubbed his face with his hands for a few seconds, and then he jumped up again and gave Jasmine a cuddle and rubbed her back.

'It never fucking rains, does it?' he said, and went to the fridge for a can of beer to wash down his sandwich.

After that Aidan was quiet for a while, living at Jasmine's and signing on, but not lifting a finger to bring any money in, not even knocking out a bit of weed like the old days. He got up in the mornings and skinned up for breakfast, then sat on the sofa drinking can after can of strong lager while staring at Heir Hunters, Loose Women and Cash in the Attic.

Jasmine saw how much he was drinking but didn't say anything. She said to Rikki that he was grieving for Nick.

'He's an alkie, love,' said Rikki. 'Look at his eyes. You can see all the little red veins. That's cos they pop, with the pressure. You want to get him dried up.'

'He just wants summat to take his mind off it,' said Jasmine, flicking fag ash over her shoulder into the sink.

The next day she came in and dumped a new Jeff Banks polo shirt on his lap. 'It's about time you thought about sprogging off,' she said. 'That Macey Kirkstone's just split up with her boyfriend. She could do with someone steady. You want to ask her out. I'll lend you a bit of cash.'

Aidan said, 'Her? She's just a kid.'

'She's seventeen. She's told Janice in the hairdresser's she's desperate for a babby. Quiet as a mouse she is. She'll see you right.'

'Christ,' said Aidan. He went upstairs and lay on his bed thinking about Suzie and tears came to his eyes, and he thought about his mum and what Jennyviv might have said, and decided to cut her some slack because she was obviously going off her nut after everything that had gone on.

He was trying to cut down on the drinking, but he needed a few cans and the odd spliff to get through the day. Jasmine would come in and see him lazing around in the same chair that Davey and then Nick had sat in, and purse her lips.

Then one day she said she was worried about Jay going off the rails, and that put Aidan's back up.

'You never bothered about the rest of us pissing our lives away.'

'No,' said Jasmine, 'But your dad and your brother hadn't just died. You pissed it away for the sheer hell of it.'

But she needn't have worried. Jay was growing up into one of those musclebound pretty boys, with more interest in waxing his chest than nicking cars or standing outside chip shops waiting to get glassed. Davey and Nick dying didn't seem to have disturbed a single hair on his Lynx-smelling head.

'That's because he's bottling it up,' said Jasmine. 'When

it comes out, it's going to be a fucking mess, and I'll have to pick up the pieces.'

Aidan told her she was talking bollocks. But maybe Jay was a bit quieter than usual, and he spent a lot of his time on his own up in his room. Aidan wondered if he should go up and have a word, but he figured Jay was probably just on the internet, and he didn't want to walk in on him having a wank.

All this time Jasmine and the boys were eating Savers baked beans and going to sleep in their clothes for the warmth, because there was eff-all money coming in and half of what there was was going to pay off Davey's benefit fraud and the fine for non-payment of car tax that Jasmine had racked up when he was ill. She said the slate should be wiped clean now Davey was dead, but unfortunately he had got her to say the fraud was her because he had a previous offence, and now the dicks at HMRC didn't seem to be interested in setting the record straight.

Jay was at Sheffield College and got some spends from working at a posh bar in town, but Aidan was still moping about the place trying not to let what had happened with Suzie tip him over the edge. The Gary Lamb dreams were getting pretty bad and once he woke up with a mouth full of blood after chewing through his lip.

'You want to get off your big fat arse,' said Jasmine, who didn't have any work herself. She had got let go from the casino kitchens for filching chicken breasts, and she was up to forty a day again. She was starting to have an old woman's wrinkled throat.

Usually when she said stuff like that Aidan didn't even reply. He just kept watching the telly or fiddling with his phone, and somehow as the weeks went by they were at daggers drawn.

Aidan had not been back at home long before he started to hear the things that Karol had been saying about Nick and Jasmine. It was mainly stuff that Jay was picking up on the estate. He had been trying not to mention it to Jasmine or Aidan because he knew they would kick off, but one day he came back from the park so angry that he let it slip.

He had been playing football and drinking cans with his mates when Karol had gone by and said something about Jasmine looking well in black. So Jay had gone for him and Karol had laid him out with one punch.

Sitting on the front step with a bag of frozen peas on his cheekbone, Jay gave Aidan the whole story. How Jasmine and Karol had slept together and that was what had made Nick so mad that he drove up the Parkway like a loon and killed himself. This was the first Aidan had heard of all that because Jasmine had glossed over her part in it and made out that the crash had been an accident.

Aidan listened calmly and then put his hand on Jay's neck, told him it would be alright and not to go for Karol again because Karol knew how to take care of himself, and the same thing would keep happening until the day Jay took a screwdriver or a steak knife with him, and that would be the day he ended up dead.

'Do we just take it, then?' said Jay.

Aidan stroked his hand over his scalp and grinned, then got up and went inside and put a couple of frozen sausage rolls in the oven.

When Jasmine got home there was hell to pay. Aidan was

raving about why didn't she tell him what had gone on, and she was saying what the fuck business was it of his who she slept with, and it all got dredged up from the year dot till Aidan slammed the front door and steamed round the estate for an hour, snapping branches off trees and kicking bins over.

When he had calmed down he came back and they were alright with each other again. They all sat round with grim faces and Jasmine said, now that Jay had told them about Karol lamping him and going around laughing about what had happened, what were they going to do about it?

'What am I going to do, you mean,' said Aidan.

'I don't mind stabbing the cunt if you're too scared to,' said Jasmine.

Jay was looking from one to the other. Jasmine was egging the pair of them on, saying Aidan wasn't much of a brother to Nick if he didn't do something about it, and if he wouldn't do it then she would, because Jay was too young to do it on his own. Jay looked miffed and relieved at the same time. But then Aidan said there was no way he was going back inside just because Nick and Jasmine had been having it off with the wrong people, and if Jay had any sense he'd leave it well alone as well. He stood up and left Jasmine sitting there with a face like a rusty nail, and after that they got on worse than ever.

Jay took the hint, though, and gave up any thoughts of jumping Karol with Davey's old replica samurai sword. He spent his time bodybuilding and trying to keep on top of his girlfriend.

36

ONE DAY AIDAN told Jasmine he had been diagnosed with liver damage, just to shit her up. The next day, when he told her it was a joke, she said it was the last chuffing straw and he could find himself somewhere else to live.

There was a flat for rent above a second-hand furniture shop and flea market on London Road. It was one of those horrible rickety old places where you paid cash and didn't get a contract, and in return they didn't ask you any questions or start trying to register you for council tax. And although you were probably breathing in enough mould spores to sink the Titanic, it was good to sit there giving the world the rods with deep house pumping out and six kebab shops within a hundred and fifty yards.

The landlord was a bald cockney called Graham. Aidan told him his name was Nath.

'As in Nathan?' said Graham, and Aidan said, 'Yep,' and then he gave Graham a fistful of grimy tenners for his first month's rent.

'No dealing from the flat,' said Graham, meaning it was fine if Aidan was a dealer, but keep it out of sight.

There were black patches of damp in the corners and the dogs next door barked all night. But Aidan liked it there. You got into the flat up an outdoor flight of stone steps from the delivery yard at the back of the shop, and once you were in it was like a fortress. There was a peephole in the door, and if he didn't like who came knocking he reckoned it would be pretty easy to open the door and give them a good hard whack with a hammer and send them sprawling all the way back down the steps to the yard.

Since Graham had given him the idea, he gave Karamat Kizil a call and started dealing a bit here and there, just dribs and drabs to cover the rent and food and a bit of spending money. He didn't know many people at this end of town so he went around as Nath, and sat about boozing at the King's Head and selling hash in the toilets.

But he was in a bit of a bad way still, after what had gone on with Suzie, and the creeps and weirdos started to gravitate towards him. He was drinking more and more, and after a couple of months he got careless.

There was a scrote called Tommy Murphy who drank in the King's Head and generally hung around the pool table picking fights. He noticed Aidan knocking out teenths and heavily cut speed to the wimps and kids and basket cases who came in there, and one night he invited Aidan to a game of pool and then got dead pally with him, buying him pint after pint of Red Stripe and offering him dabs out of this damp little bag in the bogs, as if he didn't know that Aidan had a pocketful himself.

After a bit he was getting in the large vodkas as well, and Aidan was getting a bit pie-eyed. Tommy was alright because it was dead easy, playing pool, to leave his glass first on one table and then on another, and then to get Aidan another pint in while he was in the bogs and not get one for himself. Aidan started slurring his words and staggering about, and all the other drinkers were looking at him funny, wondering whether he was going to kick off or chuck up.

After closing Tommy bought him a chicken tikka pizza, and kept giving him a guzzle on this half-bottle of gin he had in his pocket. Then he helped Aidan up the back steps of his flat and left him to it, but before he went he took the door off the latch. He gave it a good pretend slam, then sat on the steps and played a few rounds of Candy Crush on his Samsung while he waited for Aidan to doze off.

After half an hour Tommy went back up the stairs and pushed the door open, and went into the flat. He went into the main room and found Aidan passed out on the sofa, with one of the Freeview soft porn channels looping away on the telly.

He helped himself to the bag of weed lying on the table and started looking round the flat for the rest of Aidan's gear. Even though he had tried to take it easy, he was pretty pissed himself. There was nothing obvious like a plastic bag on top of the wardrobe or a box under the bed, and he didn't fancy hunting through Aidan's dirty socks on the floor. So then he looked at Aidan lying there on the sofa with his wallet bulging in the back pocket of his jeans, and the front pocket where there was probably a fistful of wraps.

He didn't much fancy Aidan waking up while he was trying to pick his pocket, and also he felt funny about putting his hand down there by another man's crotch. So he headed back to the door of the flat, and as he was about to leave he happened to see the hammer Aidan kept there in case of visitors. He picked it up and went back to the main room, weighing up whether he dared to use it, but as he got near the sofa he stumbled over some empty cans and Aidan stirred. Before Tommy could get his footing Aidan sat bolt upright and caught him by the wrist. He yanked Tommy down till his face was in the carpet and his arm was behind his back. 'Looking for something?' he said. 'Looking for something?' Then he pushed harder till they both heard the bone in Tommy's forearm snap.

Tommy screamed but on London Road in the small hours of a Saturday there are lots of screams and not many ears interested in hearing them.

Aidan said, was there a reason he should stop now or should he start thinking of more things he could do. He still had Tommy's arm bent right back and Tommy was whimpering away saying, please, please, he would keep his gob shut, please, and Aidan kept asking 'What do you reckon?', but in the end he marched him through the flat and chucked him down the stairs at the back, and Tommy lay there moaning for a few minutes and then managed to get up and go off.

Straight away Aidan figured that a piece of work like Tommy would be making an anonymous call to the police, so he emptied all his wraps on to the table and starting cutting lines like there was no tomorrow.

Sure enough, the blue flashing lights arrived, but this was three quarters of an hour later and by that time the only thing they could charge Aidan with was origami. There was a stack of unfolded papers like sweet wrappers on the table, and Aidan was lying on the floor next to it, fitting.

The ambulance crew said his heartbeat was all over the place, and it was a miracle he hadn't choked on his own vomit. They took him in and they went through all the procedures that you always did when you were committed to giving excellent care regardless of the patient's behaviour and lack of responsibility for his own welfare.

37

A FTER HE FELL out with Jasmine and went off living on his tod, everyone said that Aidan had turned into an oddball. There was something about the crumpled clothes he wore, his bad skin, and the shark-eyed stare he pushed around the junk shops and chip shops and cheapest cigs and booze in town, that made him seem a bit touched. Irene in the taxi office said he was a schizo, and the reason he trawled the junk shops was he was looking for piano wire to garrotte people with. But Gemma, whose sister Lucy had been diagnosed years back and lived in sheltered housing in Daventry, said that was prejudice pure and simple. And Brendan, who had been to Aidan's place for some ciders on Grand National day, said it was just your average loser's flat. 'No stacks of hoarded phone books, no shit smeared on the walls, no pentagrams, no cat skeletons, nothing.' He smiled at Gemma and her lovely tits, but she just rolled her eyes and said, 'Yeah, that's great.'

But there was no question Aidan was having trouble in the head. Some people said he was just a mummy's boy who had always had Jasmine to wipe his arse for him, and now that they had fallen out he was losing it like a toddler. Some people said he was a junkie and Jasmine had chucked him out for nicking her jewellery. And some people said nowt, but when they saw Aidan coming, they made sure to cross over to the other side of the road.

Whatever the truth of all that, either Aidan was an

insomniac or he was scared of dark, because his flat had no curtains and the light blazed out over the second-hand furniture shop all night every night.

'Maybe he's turned into one of those Muslim extremists, sitting up till all hours on the internet finding out how to make a bomb,' said Irene, and although no one had ever seen Aidan go into a mosque in his life, Jasmine was obviously from one of those dark-skinned countries, so you never knew.

Then Graham the landlord got to hear about Aidan having a few screws loose, and also about the dealing and what had gone on with Tommy Murphy, so he was looking for an excuse to get him out. Aidan was more trouble than he was worth, and Graham had heard that Kosovans would go two families to a room, so long as you took cash. So when the next door neighbour got in touch to say they thought Aidan was drilling a hole through the party wall, that was that. He was out on his ear, although Graham let him off the last three weeks rent.

'Just to be shot of the bugger,' he explained to Irene, who had agreed to meet him at the pub on the ring road on a steaks-for-two deal.

So then Aidan was doing the rounds on people's sofas. Since everyone was saying he had gone a bit nuts, no one wanted him about for long – it was one night and sorry, son, you're on your way.

38

T HE NEXT THING was Stuart Higginbotham, who was an old mate of Nick's, felt sorry for Aidan so he offered him a spot of cash in hand. Higgsy had a little van and ran his own business clearing people's drains.

Higgsy would lie by the open manhole and feed in a massive long rod in sections to clear the blockage. There were different attachments that went on the end that were shaped like hoes and eagle's claws and plungers and so on. The skill was knowing from the position and feel of the blockage which attachment you needed, and then rodding the drain in the right way to make it come loose. Sometimes it came in dribs and drabs and sometimes it came in a sudden torrent. When that happened it was called a 'gusher', and Higgsy knew the exact right moment to turn his head away so that he didn't get flecks of other people's shit all over his face and lips, or even leap up out of the way if it was a big one. Sometimes it would gush down so quickly that the next bit of drain couldn't cope, and the water would rise and flood over the top of the manhole with little scraps of bog paper and brown lumps floating in it.

It was usually too much paper down the bog that had caused the blockage, that or tampons. But there was the odd pair of underpants or guinea pig or whatever, and Higgsy used to shake his head and say there were some silly bastards in the world.

Usually they dealt with women because they were the ones who had to wait in while their husbands went off to jobs they thought were more important than the sewerage. But Higgsy never got his end away because of course he smelt of drains, and anyway the thought of a bloke who had come to deal with their turds was hardly going to get the housewives in the mood.

It was Aidan's job to break up the blockages after Higgsy had released them, get more rod sections from out the van, hand him attachments, and hose down the yard afterwards. If it was a really bad one then Higgsy might send him down into the drain in a pair of waders.

The work did him good, and although he stank even worse than when he was going off his nut, he started to act a bit less weird.

At the end of the day Higgsy gave Aidan thirty quid or whatever, and they went home for a long, hot shower and a change of clothes. Higgsy had spent an arm and a leg on a top-of-the-range power shower, for obvious reasons.

Aidan was sleeping in the box room. It was a three-bed house, but Higgsy's little sister was staying at the moment, working on the make-up counter at Debenhams and living it up at the weekends. Her Del was in Afghanistan and they were supposed to be saving for a big wedding, but Melody had developed a taste for ecstasy tablets and was seeing this badboy welder on the side.

One weekend, Melody's mate Jojo was down from Huddersfield for a bender. By the time Higgsy and Aidan got back from work, the girls were already halfway through a box of Bacardi Breezers, and while Higgsy was in the shower Aidan had a beer with them.

'Phwoar, you fucking stink you do,' Jojo was saying. 'Like a fucking tramp.' She kept going on about it and needling him. She had this really hostile way with her that seemed to be a clumsy version of flirting.

Melody said, 'I think she likes you,' blowing on her nails.

Aidan didn't say anything. He drained his Beck's and looked in the fridge for a scotch egg he had seen in there earlier in the week.

After Higgsy had come out of the shower Aidan went in, and when he came out he was drying his hair with his towel but had nothing covering his waist. Jojo came out of Melody's room, passed him on the landing and pointed to his privates.

'Not such a big lad after all,' she said. 'That's the sort of tiddler you're meant to throw back.'

Aidan said, 'Don't worry, it gets bigger when it's needed.'

Jojo laughed.

When he was dressed he came downstairs, and Jojo was still going on about it. Her and Melody giggled when Aidan came in, and then she started making a 'tiny cock' gesture with her little finger and saying it was no wonder he was always beating people up, he must be venting all that disappointment.

'Jesus,' said Aidan after this teasing had gone on for a while. 'You seem very interested in it. Why don't you come upstairs for an hour and then we'll see how small you think it is.'

And Melody said, 'Yeah, get a room.' At first she had laughed along with Jojo but now she wasn't laughing. Jojo was like a terrier with a rat, and it was all getting a bit much. Higgsy was going out to pick up some beer and a quarter of skunk, and Melody said she'd go with him. She was hoping to pick up some extras with the skunk and let big brother foot the bill.

After they had gone it was just Aidan and Jojo, and she kept on going on about the size of his cock, 'You poor bastard,' and so on.

'You're a real pain in the arse,' said Aidan eventually, 'you know that?'

'You would fucking love it,' said Jojo.

Then she got up and walked out of the room, looking over her shoulder at him. He followed her upstairs and grabbed hold of her from behind as she was going into Melody's room. It was a kind of a wrestle, half fight and half cuddle. She bit him while they were kissing and it fucking hurt, but he wrestled her down on to the bed and they did it.

Afterwards they sat on the bed and shared one of Melody's Marlboro Lights. 'Not so small after all, eh?' he said, then went downstairs and got them a beer each. But when he got back upstairs she was brushing her hair and she gave him a stony look.

She took the beer and had a big gulp, and then started getting dressed.

By the time Higgsy and Melody got back they were sitting downstairs as if nothing had happened, except Jojo was dead quiet.

'Alright?' said Melody, and she said, 'Yeah, fine,' and they all had another beer and a spliff before Melody and Jojo headed out for the night.

On the Saturday the girls got up about midday, and Higgsy made them coffee and Danish pastries from Lidl. The four of them sat around all day drinking beers and watching crap on the telly. Aidan tried to talk to Jojo once or twice, but she wasn't playing. It was funny how when she was being a pain in the arse he couldn't bear her, but now she was all quiet and polite he wanted her to start teasing him again.

When it got late he was hoping for a rerun of the night before, but as soon as Melody stood up to go to bed, Jojo leapt up too and said, 'I'll come with you,' and it was clear that there was nothing doing. So Aidan sat up with Higgsy instead watching *The Bourne Ultimatum*.

When he woke up in the morning the girls were gone. He ate a bowl of honey Shreddies and was just starting to think about a bath when the police turned up at the door saying something about an allegation of rape.

39

THEY TOOK HIM to an interview room like all the others he'd ever been in and asked him what had gone on the other night. Did he know Miss Joanne Somerville, was he living at present in the house of Stuart Higginbotham? Did he recall the events of Friday evening between 4.15pm and 8.30pm? Had he gone upstairs with Miss Somerville and exposed himself?

No.

Rustling of paper. 'You didn't go upstairs with Miss Somerville?'

'Not the first time. I went up for a shower. I was covered in shit.'

The other tosser, leaning in: 'Mr Wilson's been working for Mr Higginbotham's drain clearing business.'

'Has he? And is that taxable employment?'

Aidan sat there with his mouth shut. That was just a piece of bollocks they were trying to reel him in with.

'So you went upstairs for a shower. And then what?'

'And then I had a shower.'

'And then what? You called Miss Somerville upstairs?'

'No, she turned up on the landing of her own free will.'

'And that was when you exposed yourself to her.'

'Yeah.' Aidan sat back in his chair and stretched his arms like it was all no sweat. 'Not on purpose. I come out the shower drying my hair and I didn't think there would be anyone there. So she saw my cock. She had a good look at it.'

'And then–'. The copper made a show of consulting his notes. 'And then she started teasing you about the size of your genitals.'

'Yeah.'

The other one chirped up. 'I bet that pissed you off.'

'It did, yeah. But Mel said it was just cos she fancied me.'

'It was Miss Higginbotham who gave you the idea?'

'What idea?'

The coppers exchanged smiley looks, like they had him now. 'You wanted to get your own back.'

'Not really. I didn't give a shit. It was a bit annoying.'

So then they started asking about what happened later, after Higgsy and Mel had gone out.

'And, that time, you took her upstairs with you?'

'What, over my shoulder? No. She was going on about my cock again, and I says she's a pain the arse, and she says I'd love it—'

'Meaning?'

'Meaning love to fuck her, and then she goes out and gives me the come-on over her shoulder and goes upstairs, so I followed her.'

The copper went all stern and acted surprised and said, 'You followed her upstairs? Why?' and Aidan screwed up his eyebrows and said, 'To shag her.'

'So you admit that you followed Miss Somerville intending to have your way with her?'

'Yeah, that was the idea.'

'Whether she wanted to or not?'

Aidan scratched the back of his head. 'I already knew she

wanted to. That's what the look meant. That's why she went upstairs and that's why I followed. What was I supposed to do, sit there watching *Coronation Street* till she came downstairs again looking pissed off?'

'And did you?'

'Did you what?'

'Did you have sex with her?'

'Yeah.'

And so on.

While he was on remand Jay came to see him.

'Where's Mam?' said Aidan, but Jay shook his head and blushed.

'Does she think I did it? Fucking hell.' And then he went off on one till the screw gave him a warning look and Jay said not to take it out on him, it wasn't his fault. So Aidan said to tell Jasmine she'd better be there next time, she'd fucking better.

She did turn up, but you could tell as soon as you saw her face that she had decided already.

'You've done it this time,' she said.

'Oh, right,' he said sarcastically. 'That's it then, is it? Guilty verdict. Throw away the key.'

She looked at him in disgust. 'That poor cow. You've ruined her whole life, you have, just because you couldn't take no for an answer.'

'That's not how it was.'

But she wouldn't believe him. It was like this was the chance for Jasmine to vent how angry she was over Nick dying and it being a bit her fault for shagging Karol and Aidan not having the guts to go and do Karol over in revenge. Once word got round that Aidan's own mum thought he was guilty, that opened the floodgates and everyone said a filthy rapist like that should be strung up or get raped himself. 'He will, in prison,' said Irene, like she knew all about it, and took a big long suck on her Embassy No.1. And Gemma said it was disgusting, he should be shot, and Brendan said he would happily be the one to pull the trigger, all the while watching where Gemma's thighs went into her skirt and trying to get a sniff of her deodorant, and then Irene got a call from an irate customer who was waiting outside Pond's Forge, and Brendan had to scuttle off back to his minicab.

The word got round that Aidan was the lowest of the low, and if you believed everything you heard then it was a good job for Aidan that he was inside, because otherwise he would be hoisted on a pitchfork in two seconds flat. Jay was still coming to visit him and when he sat there, looking scared, Aidan asked him what was the matter. Jay told him and Aidan just laughed. 'That's all talk,' he said. 'People mouthing off. They can say what they like, but they won't do shit. Anyway I didn't do it and when I get off, because it's her word against mine, they'll all start saying she's an evil lying bitch and they'll be my best mates again.'

40

O N REMAND IT was just the same old same old. Endless ping pong and staring at the telly if you had one or if not the walls, and watching the other inmates strutting around like it meant something. Aidan's old cellmate Jake from Wakefield was back inside again too. He had helped his cousin ram raid a building society and got three years. He said it was worth it for the sight of all those cunts in suits scuttling for cover.

Jake said that when they got out Aidan should come up and stay with him in Leeds, where he could get some A-grade coke, and that would prove once and for all that West Yorkshire was where it was at. Aidan said yeah that was a good idea, and then put Michael Morpurgo in both ears and went to sleep.

He had been allocated to Jennyviv again, since last time he had been inside they had seemed to build up a rapport. He said, 'Are you going to ask me if I did it, and if what I saw before and what's in my dreams is why?'

She said: 'As you know, Aidan, whatever you say to me in these sessions is confidential, unless I believe what you say constitutes evidence of serious criminal activity, in which case I am required by law to report it.'

He said, 'Yeah, well, I didn't.'

The Michael Morpurgo tapes were Jennyviv's idea. She said he had seemed to like listening to the audiobooks before, and it would help him sleep. 'The PTSD is damaging enough,' she said, 'but sometimes when you make bad decisions it might simply be down to lack of sleep.'

Aidan said, 'Tell me a decision anyone in my family has made that isn't bad.'

During the sessions Aidan started to feel uncomfortable, because he realised he was staring at Jennyviv a lot and not really listening to what she was saying. He developed this fascination with her mouth, the way you could see some of her teeth when she spoke and the way her lip glistened with lipstick or maybe spit. So to take his eyes off her he would use a felt tip to draw pictures of devils with big hairy knobs on scrap paper. And then, when he wasn't looking at her, he found the words to tell Jennyviv all over again about all the shit that had gone on in his life and all the things he'd done which he wished he hadn't, from before the first time he was inside, and since as well. Messing up with Ashleigh was pretty near the top of the list and so was Suzie, watching her mess herself up and not doing anything to stop her, but worst of all, still after all this time, was watching the video on Gary Lamb's computer, because he remembered it every day of his life and if anything it got worse every time he relived it. 'Sometimes,' he said, 'I wish I hadn't got involved, even if it meant he was still getting away with it, because at least then I wouldn't know about it and have this dog shit in my brain.'

Jennyviv just sat there listening and looking at him, and he was glad she didn't say, what about Poppy, you saved her, or, he ought to be proud of himself, or any of that crap.

As it turned out, Aidan was right when he said that he would get off. The CPS didn't have much other than Jojo's word that the sex hadn't been consensual, and although her mate Melody tried to change her tune later, she had made it pretty clear in her first interview that Jojo had been flirting like mad.

'That doesn't mean that consent was given later,' said the eager beaver who was pushing the case.

'No,' said her boss, 'But you try getting a jury to convict.'

But the jury never got the chance, because a couple of weeks before the trial Jojo said she wasn't going to testify. The police and the CPS tried to convince her otherwise and reassure her that she would get all the support she needed, that victims were treated with great respect in court and everyone involved was specially trained to ensure she could give her evidence with a minimum of distress, but Jojo said no, she had totally gone off the idea. They were pretty sure she was just saying that because she was daunted by the prospect of giving evidence, but she wouldn't budge, so the upshot was that the charges were dropped and Aidan was free to go.

41

FOR A WHILE Aidan was staying in this halfway house for ex-cons. He rang round his old mates to see if any of them would put him up, but they'd all run out of patience with him. He ended up in Chesterfield, living with these crusties he met rooting through the bins at Tesco. They had broken in to a boarded-up terrace, and they slept in there and spent the day looking for food and making a bit of cash dealing small amounts of hash and selling on stolen goods.

It was like Stockport all over again. They would all hoover up whatever they could get their hands on: ket, tablets, acid, anything really. There was a real 'one of us is going to die in their sleep' vibe. They liked Aidan, because some local bone-heads had started giving them some hassle, and he put a stop to that by taking the chief bonehead down by the railway line and breaking his cheek bone like a stick of chalk.

It was a good summer, better than outstaying his welcome on mates' sofas. He got back to having a dab here and a line there, although he never got quite as off his face as he used to. Sometimes he got a weird feeling like Suzie was going to walk in and sit down right next to him. But she never did. He thought about getting back on a bus and going to see her, but somehow he never got off his arse to do it.

As winter came on the crusties' squat turned a bit squalid, mainly because it was so cold and they all piled on more and more clothes and didn't really wash. There was an open fireplace and they lit fires in it, but there must have been a blockage because all the smoke billowed out into the room and made your eyes sting, and made everyone's coughs worse than ever.

There was this girl Tina whose boyfriend Rob had got hit by a car on the dual carriageway when he was off his tits on acid and killed. This had happened in the spring before Aidan turned up, and she had always been quiet and kept herself to herself, but then lately she had started getting trolleyed and yapping on all night like people do when they've got a mental illness or whatever. She was a bit of a headfuck really, but everyone said she was just getting over Rob. Aidan said that getting over Rob was all very well, but it was like Tina had graduated to having full-on psychotic incidents and maybe she wouldn't just get over that on her own. Goggy, the crusty he was talking to, said that was just Aidan being a straight, and he needed to loosen up a bit. Aidan said, 'Jesus H. Christ,' and that was the end of the conversation.

Now that it was getting colder most of the people in the squat were doubling up in beds to keep warm. One night everyone was sitting round getting pissed, and this Tina was sat next to Aidan kind of flirting with him, which meant she kept propositioning him and then in the next breath saying he was an evil thug and stuff like that. She slapped his face and said sorry, pulled his hair and then begged him to pull hers back, stuff like that. At one point she got up to go out for a piss and Goggy said to Aidan that he should double up with Tina for the night, 'to keep her warm and give her some comfort, and loosen you up a bit.'

Aidan said that was a fucking stupid idea. He was thinking about Suzie and also about all that crap with Jojo. But he had also started to notice Tina's body and her smell, and now the idea was planted.

After Tina came back in and they drank more and argued and laughed, people started to go off to the other rooms to bed, and Aidan ended up sitting at the fire alone with Tina leaning her head against him, and he saw how things were going to go. So he got the good blanket off his bed pile and brought it over to hers, and they got in together.

She started to snog him and so on and he went along with it for a bit. She was a pretty girl except for being so thin and ill-looking, and while they were snogging she wasn't bending his ear with any mad talk. She bit his lip once and drew blood and laughed, but he told her off and said any more of that crap and she could eff off, and she said sorry and looked it too.

Then she was putting her hand down his pants, and he liked that, and she took off his jeans and then hers, and their naked legs ran against each other under the blankets. But then she started trying to get him to go in, and he stopped her.

'I haven't got any condoms,' he said, 'and the last thing you need is to get up the duff.' So they put their hands down each other's fronts and did it that way, and afterwards Tina bust into tears and he had to hold her and tell her it was okay for like half the night until she dropped off. He finally got an hour or so of sleep himself, and then carefully got up without waking her and left the house before it got light.

He spent the next few months drifting about, sometimes kipping in a spare bed and sometimes a doorway, then a week in a subway near the ring road, until this charity worker turned up and asked him some questions, trying to make friends. The next thing he was on some list or other, and some nights he got a bed in a hostel or the council paid for him to go in a B&B, and he only spent the odd night out of doors.

He drank a lot of cheap spirits, most of them nicked from off-licenses or taken off other poor buggers who were too drunk or ill to resist. Once you were pissed, you didn't mind that your dinner was a box of Ritz crackers and your bed was a sleeping bag on a concrete floor. The booze helped him get off to sleep, and it was only on nights when it got really cold that he woke up, and then lay there in the freezing dark, thinking about everything that had happened and wishing it hadn't.

The thing about the hostels was you could get a good wash and spruce up your clothes, so the next day you didn't stink like a tramp and you could wander about without people turning up their noses. It made shoplifting easier. Aidan strolled about with the careful stagger of someone who's always drunk, and a lot of the time he had a smile on his face. But every now and then he would bump into someone he knew and they would shake their heads and go and tell everyone how are the mighty fallen. People said that evil bastard had got his just desserts.

42

ONE DAY AIDAN got word that Wakey Jakey, his mate from prison, had been released. So he told his case worker he had got a job interview and could he have some money for a suit, and with the money he bought a pay-as-you-go mobile and gave Jake a call.

Jake met him off the train in Leeds with a bottle of Archers in a Spar bag and a packet of twenty cocktail sausages. They walked back out towards Middleton looking at girls. In the city centre there were lots of students, clueless and done out nice. Jake seemed to like them a lot. But Aidan preferred it when they got out into the estates, and the girls were more likely to be frowning or pushing prams, and they looked cheaper but somehow prettier, and didn't look away when he stared at them but gave him a fuck-off glare instead.

Jake lived in a shit old terrace with two or three other lads, his cousin and a couple of his cousin's little mates. They had beans on toast and finished off the Archers, and then Jake took Aidan off to get the coke.

He got it off this cunt called Shawsy up in Seacroft. Shawsy lived in a low-rise, the middle maisonette in a stack of three. The door at the bottom was wedged open and the ground-floor maisonette seemed to be boarded up. There was some sort of dated nasty techno, Aphex Twin or whatever, shrieking out from upstairs.

In Shawsy's flat the techno was bleeding loud, and he didn't turn it down when they went in, so Jake had to shout in his ear to say how much they were after and also to say who Aidan was. He turned and pointed at him, and Shawsy looked at him and somehow managed to acknowledge him without nodding or changing the expression on his face, and Aidan did the same back.

There were a couple of other lads sat about, one a bald guy in a tracksuit who looked as if he was completely monged out and one playing Resident Evil 2 on the PlayStation, pounding the controller like it was his cock and letting a spliff burn out in the ashtray in front of him. They didn't even seem to notice that Jake and Aidan were there at all.

Shawsy sorted out the coke and they had a line there and then, to be polite. Shawsy was drinking shots of gin and bitter lemon, but he didn't offer it round. As they left he shouted in Jake's ear, 'Don't shut the door at the bottom. Lock's knackered.'

The coke was certainly worth the hassle of travelling across Leeds. They bounced their way back to Jake's flat where he cut them another line, and two each for his cousin and his pals so they could catch up. His cousin had been out to the Spar and bought twenty-four Carling and a couple of bottles of port, and they put on some Johnny Cash and sat down to get blitzed. After a while they went out to the pub and drank Stella and played pool for three hours. Then Jake's cousin threw up in the corridor on the way to the bogs, and they came home via the Spar and kept hoovering up the coke.

The next day they got up at two and went to a Wetherspoons where they had Guinness to soak up the coke and two meals for a fiver each. They were taking it in turns to go to the bogs, passing the coke between them, till the bouncers came on shift at six and started to cotton on. Then they went from bar to bar getting more and more fucked. Eventually Jake put a piece of loose kerb through a taxi window for the sheer joy of it, and had to peg it. If he had got arrested, he would have gone back inside. Aidan and Jake's cousin and his mates hung around, called his mobile but got no response, and in the end they went back to his place to finish off the coke.

The next morning there was still no sign of Jake. His mobile was going straight to answerphone. They got some beans and sausages and white bread from the Spar, went back and cooked it all.

In the evening they drank cider and passed round a bottle of poppers till they all had stinking headaches. Then the others started to pester Aidan about going round to Shawsy's for more coke.

'You don't want any more of that shit,' he said. 'Two nights is enough. Give yourselves a break.'

Jake's cousin said they would go themselves, but Aidan was the only one who knew where Shawsy lived. Aidan said this was probably why Jake hadn't told them, because they didn't know how to control themselves.

'Who are you, my dad?' said Jake's cousin.

They messed around drinking cider and arguing so long that in the end they had to go out to the Spar for more booze, and since they were out they thought they may as well call in at the pub for a couple before closing time. They got settled in a booth and hid the bags of bottles under their seats, drank tall glasses of lager and pestered Aidan about the coke.

They kept on at him until he agreed to go, but he said he had a bad vibe about the whole thing. 'This is the sort of night that goes tits up,' he said, 'and like as not it'll be my tits getting the chop.'

There was a lock-in at the pub, and they didn't stagger out into the street till nearly two. Then Jake's cousin and his mates went off towards Jake's house to wait, and Aidan set off in the direction of Shawsy's house.

It took him a while to find it again, partly because he took a wrong turn past a curry house and stopped for a bite to eat, but eventually he arrived at the little block of maisonettes, with the door propped open and the boarded-up bottom flat and the nasty techno coming from upstairs.

Everyone at Shawsy's were completely off their faces. There were seven of eight of them, smoking bongs and snorting coke, nattering on to each other over the relentless techno. In the middle of the living room a couple of dudes were melting U2 CDs over a fire in a biscuit tin. The bald guy, still wearing the same tracksuit, saw Aidan and gave him the finger from where he was sprawled on the sofa, making a deranged angry face like some kind of neo-Nazi. Aidan went from room to room looking for Shawsy, and found him lying on a mattress in one of the bedrooms. A girl was trying to give him a blow job but he was too out of it to get a hard-on. His eyes were rolling around in their sockets. It was obvious Aidan wouldn't get any sense out of him. He went back to the living room.

The techno was like the shearing of rusty metal, done over and over again five times too loud in the wimpiest part of your ear. You were always about to look down and see your guts spurt out of your belly from sheer nasty noise, but you never did. The only light came from the decks and mixer, the silent prancing and fangs of some crap horror film on the telly, an orange-bulbed lamp in the corner, and the fire in the biscuit tin flaring up in the middle of the room. The dudes stoking it looked like devils.

The flames were halfway up to the ceiling now. Someone had chucked on a little cushion. The sponge inside had caught, and the plastic of the CDs was really melting now in the heat.

The devil dudes were shouting and laughing. Aidan tried to pull one of them to one side and shouted in his ear about buying some coke, but he just stared at him with an expression that said he didn't know what the fuck was going on and he didn't care in the least what Aidan was saying. So Aidan looked on the coffee table, which had been pushed to the side of the room to make way for the fire, and found a pile of wraps. He helped himself to a few and put some notes down on the table, and left.

As he went out at the bottom of the stairwell he kicked away the doorstop holding the door open, and pulled it to behind him.

Jake was there when he got back to the house, eating a microwaved pie and watching *Die Hard with a Vengeance*. It was four in the morning. His cousin and his mates were curled up asleep, one on the sofa, one in the spare room and one in the hall using the bottom stair as a pillow. Aidan put the coke on the table and went through to put the kettle on. Apparently Jake had spent the last twenty-four hours in bed with this girl from Wombwell.

'She was dead keen,' he said. 'Kept bringing me bottles of Beck's and asking me my favourite film, and then how I wanted to do it next. She had a degree in fine art.'

'Fuck me,' said Aidan.

43

A DAY OR so later they heard there had been a big fire up in Seacroft. Presumably the biscuit tin had got out of hand, and the whole block had gone up. Everyone in the other stairwells had got out okay, but the knackered lock in Shawsy's stairwell meant they had to smash the window and jump out. One lad had broken both his legs but the others had landed on top of him and they were alright, except for some smoke inhalation. But Shawsy and the bird who had been giving him the blowjob hadn't made it out of the bedroom and they were dead. And the people living in the maisonette on the top floor, a young woman and her baby, were also killed.

As soon as Jake heard this he started looking at Aidan in a strange way, and he disappeared into the bathroom for a talk with his cousin.

'Either you're a very close family,' said Aidan when they came out, 'or you're looking to do me a bad turn.'

They accused him of setting fire to Shawsy's flat deliberately.

'Why would I do that?' he asked, and they said, because he was a nutcase.

Jake's cousin's little mates skulked about like voles, and one or other of them kept melting away and coming back a while later.

'Where's he going?' Aidan kept asking, and the answer was always, to buy some bogroll, to sign on, to fetch his girlfriend's methadone, or whatever. Then after a bit the vole would come back eating a pack of Monster Munch, but there was still nothing to wipe your arse on.

'If you're going to grass me up for something I didn't do, like the A-Team,' said Aidan after a while, 'then if I were you I'd make sure it doesn't backfire. If the police turn up and find all that coke lying around, you'll be back inside quicker than you can say "daft bastard".'

They scowled at him, but soon after Jake's cousin picked up the wraps and naffed off, for good this time, with both of his mates.

Jake said, 'I'm not going to grass you up, but you're a fucking sicko murderer, and I'm going to make sure everyone knows it.'

'Lightweight,' said Aidan. 'Get yourself round to Lady Picasso's house. She'll kiss it better.'

The upshot was that Jake and his cousin went around telling everyone that Aidan was an arsonist and had burned Shawsy to death deliberately. The rumours spread from Leeds to Sheffy. Then that Madison and her mum let on what he had said about burning down their house, and that was the clincher. People said that a baby killer like that ought to be strung up by the balls and burnt alive himself. Wherever he went, in Leeds or back in Sheffy, people looked at him as if he smelt of dog shit, barmen would pretend not to see him, and grown men would mutter threats and insults so he could half hear them, even if they didn't dare give him the pasting they said he deserved.

Of course, not everyone knew who he was, so Aidan just started drinking in other places. He was topping up his dole helping these Romanian lads take the lead off church roofs, and selling it to Davey's old mate Dwayne down the scrapyard. After a hard night's work he would go back to this lad Tomasz's house for a garlic sausage breakfast and a snooze. Tomasz lived there with his family. His dad was in charge of the operation, although he didn't come on the jobs and Aidan didn't see him much.

It was obvious that Tomasz's sister had a crush on him. The way she watched him. It was flattering, and he started to fancy her back, which was a problem because she was only fifteen. Aidan didn't want to take advantage, but he thought about Elise more and more, and he was starting to think he would have to move on if he didn't want to ruin Elise's life and end up in a ditch himself, shot in the back of the head by Elise's father.

He would sit in the pub all afternoon feeling glum and picking over the scab of everything, worrying that he was going to turn out like Gary Lamb. Now that he was out of prison and had stopped talking to Jennyviv, the nightmares and black moods and wetting the bed were as bad as ever.

Then one day a couple of coppers walked in and came straight over to his table.

'Mr Aidan Wilson?' said the WPC.

'Are you the stripper I ordered?' said Aidan. He couldn't help himself. They were going to arrest him anyway, but now they handled him all the more roughly.

'Hope you don't struggle and require the pepper spray,' said the WPC as they palmed him into the car, but in the event they must have decided it wasn't worth the paperwork, because they let him off with a knee in the bollocks on the way to the cells.

In the interview room they asked if he had been at Mr Shaw's house on the night in question.

'It's a maisonette,' he said.

'Was,' said the detective.

Aidan said they knew he had been there because everyone in South and West Yorkshire seemed to know all about it, and anyway he expected they had found his fingerprints all over the place. 'And I don't see any reason to pretend I wasn't there either.'

They asked what he had been doing there, and he thought for a while and then said, 'I went to buy some coke.'

The detective said, 'Wouldn't that violate the terms of your licence?' and Aidan said, 'Yes, if I'd actually got some, but they wouldn't let me have any.'

'Why not?'

'Because they were dicks. They were off their faces. It was half house party and half orgy and half satanic ritual.'

The fat detective sat back and dug some wax out of his ear. 'So when they wouldn't sell you any cocaine, you locked them in and torched the place.'

'No. They already had the fire going when I arrived. Stupid bastards. It wasn't my fault.'

'You didn't stop them, though.'

Aidan shrugged.

'And you did lock them in.'

They showed Aidan the CCTV from the forecourt outside the block. It showed him arriving. Then they fast-forwarded to the bit where he came out again. At the doorway you could see him kicking away the doorstop and pulling the door closed, then walking off.

'What did you do that for?'

'I didn't think it was safe, leaving the door propped open like that. In the middle of the night. For the people in the other flats. To have cunts like me walking in and out. Breaking in, robbing the place.'

'So you locked them in. As a public service.'

'Yeah. I shut the door. I didn't lock them in.'

'Did you know the lock was broken? And they couldn't get out once you'd shut it.'

Aidan thought about this for a few seconds. 'No.'

'We have a witness who says you did.'

Then they asked him about what he had said to Madison's mum, but he said that was a load of bollocks, and since it was his word against hers, and she had a vendetta against him for treating Madison like shite, it wasn't much in the way of evidence.

They held him for a day or so, and then they let him go. No one was ever charged for any offence in relation to the fire, but Aidan said he would rather have been charged, because then it would have been settled one way or the other. As it was, people blamed him for the deaths, because Jake and his cousin had gone about spreading shit about him, because of his reputation, and because he had been stupid enough to shut the door at the bottom of the stairs.

44

AIDAN THOUGHT IT was best not to go back to stripping lead with Tomasz, because sooner or later he and Elise would end up in the house alone together, and he didn't want to lie in a schoolgirl's bed. So he hopped on a bus to Worksop, where that kid Joe, who had grown up down the street, was living now.

Joe worked in a tropical fish shop. He had never really got over the kicking that Shelley Turner and Mark Crabbe had given him, but maybe that was a good thing. Instead of getting shot full of holes in Afghanistan, he was doling out neon tetras in North Notts. He told Aidan he could sleep on the sofa for a week or so, 'but I don't want any trouble. Things are going OK for me here.'

Joe had a girlfriend, called Jayne, who was into the Smashing Pumpkins, a black nail varnish type. This was what happened to Goths when they grew up. She was a tattooist, and apparently she had a smoking Smith & Wesson on her inner thigh. She made her own Blastaways using cider, white wine and fruit juice. 'It's not the same,' she said, 'but it keeps me happy.'

'She's five years older than me,' Joe told Aidan.

'I like her,' said Aidan. 'I mean, I don't fancy her, but I like her. It just shows that going to college doesn't necessarily turn you into a knobend.'

'Thanks,' said Joe.

There was a rat problem in Joe and Jayne's back yard. Aidan spent half his days sitting in wait with a catapult near a pile of flour, and whenever a rat ventured out for a nibble, which was about once every four hours, he'd take a shot. It was a complete waste of time, but it filled the days while he waited for Joe and Jayne to get back from work.

Sometimes he got bored, and popped out for a stroll round Worksop, to see what he could see.

One day, about three weeks after he arrived, he came out of the house and straight away a couple of men got out of a car parked opposite. One of them had a camera. He leant on the car and started taking pictures of Aidan. The other one walked across the road, half brash and half uncertain, and spoke to him: 'Hello Aidan. It's Aidan, isn't it?'

Aidan stopped and looked at him. The man's eyes flicked down to Aidan's fists, which were clenched but down by his sides.

'Can I have a quick word? About the fire?'

'Piss off,' said Aidan, and started walking again.

The man followed him along the pavement, saying there was a lot of talk going round about how Aidan had locked the door and left those people there, and even though he hadn't been charged and everyone in the know knew he was innocent – the dude was smiling like a suck-up – it would do Aidan good to tell his side. 'I'm sure you think about it a lot. That poor baby and her mother. You mustn't blame yourself.'

'I don't.'

'I'm afraid others do.'

The man was standing in Aidan's way now. He put his

hand out to touch Aidan's arm, but before it got there Aidan had batted it away and flicked out his fist at the man's nose.

It was only a little punch, but there was a lot of blood. The guy was laid on the pavement rolling round like an up-side-down turtle, moaning and groaning, and his mate stood on the other side of the road taking pictures. Aidan walked off.

That afternoon he got into a grudge match at the snooker club, won 12-9, and completely forgot about the prat in the street. He took a bottle of vodka back to Joe and Jayne's house, and they had kebab meat and chips for tea and drew ideas for tattoos over a few bifters. Jayne got really stoned and started telling Aidan about how she was into anal, but he went quiet and concentrated on his design for a crocodile attacking a gazelle.

A couple of days later, the shit hit the fan. There was an article in one of the tabloids about the fire that killed Shawsy and the others. It had a photo of Aidan coming out of Joe's house looking thick and cross, and the subheading asked, 'What has this man got to hide?'

The reporter was careful not to say that Aidan had lit the fire or was responsible for the deaths, but he managed to imply it very strongly by saying how Aidan had moved about since it happened, had admitted that he 'deliberately' shut the door with the faulty lock, and had refused to answer any questions. He didn't mention the fact that Aidan had split his nose from top to bottom, though he did say that he had become 'animated and aggressive when challenged.'

All in all the article said nothing that wasn't already es-tablished fact except describing very vaguely the reporter's visit. But the overall effect was to brand a big 'GUILTY' on Aidan's forehead.

'If you had money, you could sue their arse off,' said Joe.

'If he had money, they wouldn't have printed it,' said Jayne.

Aidan said it was no big deal, but Joe said it was more complicated than that.

The thing was, Jayne was a member of the local BNP.

'It's nothing to do with you being half Paki,' she said. 'It's not a racist party. Anyway, you don't look it.'

'Right,' said Aidan.

The problem was this article in the paper. The one that made out Aidan burnt babies. Sooner or later it would come out that he was staying with party members.

'Member,' corrected Joe.

Then, the way they twisted things. It would be, 'BNP thugs shelter arsonist,' and 'Maisonette murders and the far-right connection.' It wouldn't look good. So – they knew, Jayne and Joe, that Aidan was a good person, but the local party bigwigs said he had to go.

'When you say bigwigs, do you mean that dick with the mullet down at the snooker hall?'

Apparently he was called Barry. Apparently Barry was Jayne's ex.

'You want to watch him,' said Aidan to Joe, 'ordering her around.'

'Don't worry,' said Joe. 'If he ever tries to shag her, I'll give you a call and you can come and beat him up.'

There was something sarky in the way he said it. Aidan gave him a funny look, but no more was said.

The next day Aidan got on a bus and headed up to Batley to stay with Ryan.

'How's things?' said Ryan when he arrived.

'I've only got myself to blame,' said Aidan. 'If you go to

a toilet like Worksop, you've got to expect to get shat on.'

The day after that, the BNP released a statement saying that Aidan Wilson had been ordered out of town. 'Worksop's a decent place,' said spokesman Barry French. 'Let this man go back and face justice in Leeds.'

45

RYAN MANAGED TO get Aidan some work putting up plasterboard for a builder mate of his.

'It's grunt work,' said his mate. 'Any cunt can do it, as long as he can swing a hammer.'

'Oh, he can do that,' said Ryan. 'He's built like a brick shithouse, our Aidan.'

In fact he was a bit too frisky with the hammer, and there was more wastage than usual because of Aidan knocking lumps out of the panels, imagining Joe and Jayne's faces. But Ryan's builder mate put up with it, because Aidan kept himself to himself and was worth three of his usual gumbos when there was a pile of hardcore to be shifted.

Aidan slept on the sofa in Ryan's flat. In the mornings Ryan would have a shower and then walk about the flat making toast and ironing a shirt while Aidan squeezed the last drop of sleep out of the night.

One morning his sleeping bag had slipped down and his chest and arms were on display.

'Christ,' said Ryan. 'Look at your arms. They're like a couple of anacondas. No wonder you've given out a few pastings in your time.'

Aidan rolled over and yawned. 'You wouldn't set out to get pissed with a can of Shandy Bass. I only do what I've got a talent for.'

Ryan said, 'You'd be better off if you were a wimp.'

'Like you, you mean. Show us your arms.'

So Ryan did. He had a slim build. Aidan laughed and said, 'They're like candles. They're like them fucking breadsticks. I bet women are scared to cuddle you, in case they snap them!'

'I daresay they are,' said Ryan. 'But that only makes them want to cuddle me all the more.'

He put his shirt on and went to work.

All year Ryan was on at Aidan about making it up with Jasmine.

'You knacked it with Davey. Never had a chance to say goodbye or owt, and now it's too late.'

'It's not something I lose any sleep over.'

Ryan nodded. 'I'll give you that. He was a waste of space. But your mam's alright. You want to sort it out with her. You'll need her again before too long.'

Aidan made a face and sat back and fiddled with his bollocks. It seemed like he couldn't be told. But Ryan's words meant something, what with his own mam dying when he was a tiddler. His drip-drip approach must have worked, because in October Aidan said he was sacking off the plasterboarding and going back to Sheffy.

He arranged to meet Jay in a greasy spoon to see how the land lay. Jay had moved out of Jasmine's because he had got this girl knocked up. They had a flat on the fourth floor of Hanover House, and although he said he didn't love Shana any more, they were still shagging.

'What's the baby called?' Aidan asked, and Jay said, 'Kasey.'

Aidan said, 'Is that a boy or a girl?'

The breakfasts came, and Aidan and the waitress were giving each other the eye.

'What about my extra chips?' he said.

'Just coming,' she said.

While she was walking away he said just loud enough to hear, 'Nice arse,' then not quite loud enough, 'Ginger though.'

'You fucking what,' she said.

He said, 'And these beans are cold.' And so on.

After a bit he asked Jay about whether their mam would let him move back in. Jay said, 'Oh aye, she's been sticking her lip out for months. I reckon she'll be made up.' Apparently Jasmine knew all about the fire but she hadn't said anything about it either way, which Jay reckoned meant she was willing to overlook it. He texted Jasmine some yarn about bumping into someone who had been in touch with Aidan and maybe Aidan would pop in when he was around. And Jasmine texted back, 'If u like.'

So Aidan and Jay went back to Jasmine's via the pizza place and played on the Xbox till Jasmine came in from her afternoon shift at the Cutlers Arms. She and Aidan nodded at each other and said, 'Alright,' quietly, like that was the only apology either of them was going to give.

Jasmine put the shopping away and stuck the kettle on, and then breezed through saying, 'If you think a couple of meat feasts are going to make everything okay then you've got another think coming,' but the next minute she handed Aidan a mug of tea and sat down next to him, and they turned the Xbox off and watched one of the *Saw* films they had on recordings.

After that it all settled down a bit, and Aidan seemed to be the happiest he had been in a long time. Jay had a word with his supervisor at Morrisons, and got Aidan a job rounding up trolleys in the car park. Obviously, with his record, he was on probation, but he kept his head down and stuck it out, only drank a few cans in the week and stopped the weed completely. Sometimes you could see him in the park, standing dead still like he was doing tai chi, or lifting up full wheelie bins, and generally acting like a wacko who was cheerful enough and probably just a bit lonely. He started collecting up litter and putting it in the bins, and that was helpful, but the language he used to members of the public was a bit choice so the city council's Streetforce area team leader asked him to pack it in.

At the weekends he was downing a gallon of lager and a load of Aftershocks and vodka and Red Bulls before passing out in a hallway or club toilet or someone's front room, but then who wasn't?

All the talk about the fire had been dying down, and although Aidan was notorious across the estate and half of Leeds and Sheffy, the redtops had lost interest and there was no longer much danger of a lynch mob bursting through the front door to string him up. It was ages since he had got into a scrap or upset anybody. Some people said he was calming down at last, and some people said Jasmine was breastfeeding him again even though he was a grown man, and he was getting the benefit of her antidepressants. If you stood outside at night you could see he still slept with the light on, or at least lay there staring round the room at his old posters trying not to let the bad thoughts win. But he seemed happy enough in the daytime, so everyone breathed a sigh of relief and left him to it.

Jasmine said, the week after Aidan moved back in, 'I heard about that fire and that. It's fucking terrible, but it weren't your fault. I know you'd never do owt to hurt a kid.' So after that they were more solid than ever.

The months went by without Aidan breaking anyone's face or getting sacked from Morrisons, and it started to look like he was getting his life back on track. Jasmine even said to him about Macey Kirkstone again, who still hadn't sprogged off and Janice at the hairdresser's said was one in a million. But Aidan made a face that meant, leave it, so Jasmine shut her gob and didn't mention it again. A while later it turned out that Macey Kirkstone had twelve grand of credit card debt, and to take care of it she cooked up a personal injury claim with that ex of hers. She was walking around in a collar for weeks, and even though everyone knew it was put on, she still got two grand after fees. But she spent it on a holiday to Magaluf instead of putting it towards the debt, and Janice at the hairdresser's started saying she wasn't one in a million, she was a silly cow like every bugger else.

Jay was always at the gym. More and more tats were gradually creeping up his arms like a blue-green rash. It wasn't long before he had a full-on sleeve.

'They look rate they do,' said Aidan when he came back with the hieroglyphic tiger's head with the Celtic symbol for compassion underneath, or whatever the fuck it was meant to be.

'Cheers,' said Jay. 'You should have one yourself.'

But Aidan didn't fancy having a needle stuck in his arm. The very thought of it made him remember Suzie, and then he felt cobwebs all over his face and had to go for a run to stop his hands trembling and his headache coming on.

Jay prowled around all the time with a bare chest and keks that slipped halfway down his arse. When he clenched his muscles you could see all these bumps and valleys strain into shape. Aidan said it was like living in a porno.

'You won't be starring in any,' said Jay, 'with a gut like that.' He poked Aidan's belly with the end of his snooker cue.

It was true that Aidan was getting a bit podged. It was all the booze he was pouring down his throat. There was a sack of flab starting to grow all over his arms and chest, and when he clenched his muscles they didn't strain, they quivered. He laughed. 'That's called not giving a shit and being thirty-odd. I could still give you a pasting.'

Jay didn't argue with that. But later on he started pestering Aidan to come with him down the gym. 'There's loads of birds,' he said.

But Aidan just smiled out the side of his face. 'You're alright. I'll just sit here with my cans.' Then something occurred to him. He sat up straight. 'Here, can you get hold of any of them anabolic steroids?'

'That's the last fucking thing you need,' said Jay.

Aidan started to find pushing trolleys round Morrisons car park and smiling at people at bit boring, and it didn't pay well either. One day he called round Tomazs his Romanian friend's house to ask if there was any work nicking cables. Tomazs wasn't there, but his sister Elise was. She was seventeen now, or as good as.

She invited him in and then said Tomazs was on his way back from Dronfield.

'What's he doing there?' said Aidan.

'Who cares?' said Elise, and put her hand on his face. She said, 'We haven't got long,' so they trotted up to her bedroom and did it quickly. Elise said 'Ow' a bit and screwed up her face but told him to keep going or Tomazs might come back.

Afterwards Aidan said, 'Sorry, I'd have got you ready a bit more if we'd had time.'

She said it was alright, and then he asked, what if she got pregnant.

'I don't mind,' she said.

By the time Tomazs came in they were having a mug of tea in the living room. Tomazs had picked up a Chinese on the way home and he asked Aidan to stay and share it, so the three of them sat around chomping on beef chow mein like nothing had happened. Aidan asked Tomazs about the work, but he wasn't keen – it was easier with lads who didn't speak English and didn't have UK records, because they could just play dumb, give false names and disappear back to Romania when they got police bail. When Aidan left, Elise was giving him the eye over Tomazs's shoulder, and afterwards he always meant to call her but he never did.

That winter, Aidan bumped into Connor's brother Carl who he had stayed with in Nottingham a few years back. Carl had stopped taking quite so many drugs, and now he was training to be a driving instructor. They met up in the Royal Oak, this gastropub where Carl's fiancée Debs was the kitchen manager. 'What happened to whatshername? Your daughter.'

Carl's face went dark. 'Trixie. Don't see her much. Her mum makes it difficult. They live in Plymouth, and Debs gets carsick, so . . .'

Carl had turned into the sort of person who paid his TV licence. Aidan did his best to get on Carl's wavelength, but there was nothing coming back the other way. It was two minutes of awkward chat and five of watching Carl play Hungry Shark Evolution on his phone.

Then it came out that Debs had heard all about the fire and also the thing with Jojo, and she had told Carl she didn't want him seeing Aidan ever again after today.

'Dump your mates, is it?' said Aidan, and Carl stared down at his phone again. So Aidan got up and walked out.

46

S OME SOFT SODS, like Gemma at the taxi office, said it was a shame, seeing how well Aidan was getting on, that there had to be an inquest into the deaths of the four people in the fire in Leeds. It raked things up again and reminded everyone that he was some kind of demonic monster who they wanted dead.

'You callous bastard,' said Ali at the newsagents. 'It's your sort of filth that gives us Asians a bad name.' He could say what he liked because everyone knew he kept a Stanley knife by the till.

'Ten Number Ones and a scratchcard,' said Aidan. Then he wandered up the aisle to get a Pot Noodle. It was water off a duck's back.

He was called as a witness at the inquest. For a while he said that he couldn't be arsed to go, but Ryan spoke to him on the phone and told him he would look guilty as hell if he didn't turn up. Aidan said he didn't care how it looked.

'You don't make things easy for yourself, do you?' said Ryan.

'I don't make things easy for other people.'

'Numpty.'

But Aidan mulled it over, and when the time came he was there at the coroner's court.

It was the sort of inquest that people got excited over. When the woman from the fire investigation team said that someone had lit a plastics fire in a biscuit tin in Mr Shaw's flat, there was a ripple round the court that it must have been arson. And because everyone knew Aidan had locked the door at the bottom, surely that meant murder? But the coroner said that just because someone had lit a fire deliberately, this didn't in itself mean arson. Otherwise arson would be committed every day by people lighting fires in the grate.

The public gallery looked at him blankly. Nobody there had an open fire in their house.

Moreover it remained to be established who had lit the fire in the biscuit tin. No one who was in the flat at the time would now admit to it, but frankly the coroner didn't find the evidence of any one of them reliable. Perhaps they were lying, or perhaps they had been too inebriated to remember.

Mr Bartholomew (who was the bald guy in the tracksuit who had eyeballed Aidan) said that Mr Wilson had lit the fire. Perhaps that was true; but in that case, why had Mr Bartholomew not stopped him, or doused the flames when Mr Wilson left the building? It was all a little unconvincing.

And it wasn't the purpose of the court to test the motivation of Mr Wilson. He said that he had shut the door for the security of other residents, and could not remember being told that the lock was faulty. Testing the truth of that would be the task of a future criminal trial, if there was one. The coroner recorded a verdict of death by misadventure for Mr Shaw and Ms Phillips (the girl he had been in bed with), because they had been revellers at the party in which the fire had been lit, and accidental death for Ms Hardacre and her baby in the flat upstairs.

It was amazing how suits could talk in this bullshit way even when they were telling you how your children died.

That was a strand of the anger the families felt then, but mostly their hatred was focused on Aidan Wilson sitting there bold as brass in his Adidas tracksuit and matching trainers.

The parents of Anna Phillips, the girl who had been trying to suck some life into Shawsy's coke-limp cock, were angry at the verdict of death by misadventure. The Phillipses lived in a big house out by Crosspool. It was bad enough that their daughter had died in such a place. It was hard enough to imagine their bright girl Anna, who had been accepted to read English at Exeter, lying on a mattress with this drug dealer, and this being the place where she had suffocated to death through smoke inhalation. But the idea that somehow she had been an accomplice in her own death, a willing party to the stupid madness of the biscuit tin, when in fact she had been lying in bed in another room and a victim of what had happened, innocent in all senses of the word, made their blood boil.

But they said nothing about any of this to Aidan, or anyone else at the court except their calm solicitor. He listened and then took them away to a room where he explained the verdict in more detail and explained their options going forward. And then they went off and lived the rest of their ruined lives – the depression, the divorce, his death on a golf course and her remarriage to a Scottish geography teacher who had been widowed in a ferry disaster. Aidan never saw or heard of them again.

Shawsy's sister Vicky was a bit more vocal. As soon as the coroner gave his verdict she started screaming at Aidan that he was a murderer and tried to scramble from one side of the gallery to the other to get at him.

'You've broke me mam's fucking heart!' she wailed. Her mother was there in the space reserved for wheelchairs, wearing an oxygen mask for her emphysema, and the only way she could express her anger was by coughing and coughing. Her cheeks, or what you could see of them outside the mask, were wet with tears, but whether this was because of grief or because of the coughing was anyone's guess.

Vicky was completely beside herself. 'When Sean gets back he'll rip your head off. I'll fucking kill you myself. I'll get you with a carving knife.'

Her kids were sat looking up at her, and their stepdad was trying to hold her back and calm her down. He was chucking in the odd, 'You'd better watch yourself, pal,' to be supportive, but he was licking his lips and looking nervous, scoping out whether Aidan was going to leap over the seats and pummel him.

Aidan looked at them and then at bald Bartholomew, who had said he lit the fire, looking daggers back at Aidan. Aidan didn't seem bothered. He kept sitting there till Vicky ran out of steam and the rest of her family shepherded her out. After a minute her bloke came back in to wheel out his mother-in-law. You could still hear Vicky's anguished swearing echoing in the high-ceilinged waiting room outside.

The other family were a bit more controlled. The girl, Liz Hardacre, had fallen out with her family over a man. The man was a footballer in League Two and Liz had met him at one of the parties she used to get invited to at Nottingham Marina. Her dad was the boss of Hardacre Construction, one of those building firms that did a lot of medium-sized contracts with local authorities and did a lot of subcontracting and moving premises. It was the sort of outfit that went bankrupt one month and started up with a slightly different name the next. Iffy as.

So darling Liz had got used to drinking cava and hanging around with the rich set, and that's where she had met her footballer. And daddy hadn't approved because he said the pillock would get her in the club and then be on his way, so she had stormed off saying he was a bully and a control freak. And of course she had got pregnant and the pillock had dropped her like a stone. She had ended up in a council maisonette, too proud to go back to her dad, with a collicky baby and postnatal depression. And after six months of that she had burned to death.

The footballer had broken his leg in a car accident, been found to be over the limit, and had his contract terminated. Last anyone heard he was living in East Anglia, shovelling shit at a turkey farm where they raised 140,000 birds a year.

Bob Hardacre waited till the Shaw family had shot their load, and then he walked up and spoke to Aidan when he was getting up to go.

'I know you're to blame for my daughter's death,' he said, and then his face nearly crinkled up and he added, 'and my granddaughter's.'

Aidan looked at him and said nothing.

'If you hadn't been there, they'd still be alive.'

'That's probably true,' said Aidan.

'And I don't buy that shit about the door lock.' He jabbed his finger at Aidan's chest. 'You knew exactly what you were doing. You're a fucking murderer.' His face was all red and he was losing control of his voice.

Aidan said, 'I wish I hadn't locked the door. I'm sorry they died, but it wasn't my fault.' And he looked Bob full in the face, and then stepped past him and walked out of the court. Bob Hardacre clenched his teeth and burst into tears, and his wife had to help him out to the waiting area where an usher got him a plastic cup of water.

That was show over for the day.

After the inquest, the Shaw family, bald Bartholomew, and Bob Hardacre put it about that Aidan was responsible for the killings and had only got away with it for lack of evidence. The coroner had said that Aidan's version of events was highly questionable, and people were going around saying he had called Aidan a liar, which was almost like saying he had done it. The worst of it was that Vicky Shaw lived not far away in Sheffield, so her stirring really got things going on the estate. The fuss and gossip over the fire and Aidan's involvement in it flared up worse than ever. People said that Aidan would get what was coming to him, either at the hands of Sean Shaw or Bob Hardacre's dubious associates, or just by walking into a pub where there happened to be some hard nut who was willing to take him on.

The supermarket gave him his P45 and although they said it was because of the bad language he had used to that city councillor, you could just tell it was because the bastards didn't want it getting around that they were employing public enemy number one. Aidan was all for doing his own version of *Supermarket Sweep* with a pick mattock and a tin of paint, but Jay said then he would lose his job too and couldn't Aidan just fuck off for once and not spoil it for the rest of us?

Even people on the estate who had known him for years turned against him. They said they were ashamed that someone from round there would torch innocent people. He was bringing the estate into disrepute. Carl and his stuck-up fiancée Debs had already made their feelings plain. Carl's brother Connor said he didn't know about the fire, but the way Aidan hadn't come back for his dad's funeral, or even for Nick's, was disgusting. Carl and Connor turned into Aidan's worst enemies overnight, telling everyone he had always been unhinged, and half the stuff he'd done hadn't even come out yet.

Aidan started going in the Royal Oak just to wind Carl up. When Debs came out of the kitchen to say the chicken goujons had run out or to field a complaint about underdone pork, Aidan would raise his glass and leer at her. One night he stayed in the lounge drinking double gins until throwing out time, and then waited in the car park till Debs came out.

'What do you want with me?' she said as she hurried past him to her terracotta Beetle.

'Ask Judas,' said Aidan, looming over her like a grizzly bear.

She would have maced him but her hands were trembling too much to get it out of her handbag. She sat in the car with the doors locked and sobbed.

Ian the bouncer, who had had to give up working the doors since his hernia operation, went around the estate telling people Aidan was a menace and they should petition the council to get him evicted.

Gemma said she didn't know, maybe it was all those blows to the head that had made Aidan's brain work funny. It turned out Gemma liked watching boxing, and that seemed somehow pervy for a girl. Brendan said, 'I used to be a welterweight,' but Gemma just laughed.

Irene said this whole area wanted knocking down and starting again.

47

ONE TIME AIDAN borrowed Jay's Golf and drove up to the prison where he had done his time. He sat and watched the cars coming and going, and eventually clocked Jennyviv going by in a dark green Saab.

The next day he did the same again, only this time he followed her.

She drove out to one of the leafy suburbs like he knew she would, all avenues with black-and-white bay windows and double garages and paved driveways and security lights. It was the sort of place you could turn over and get enough to live on for a week, even just selling shit round the back of the pub or in the stairwells of one of the tower blocks. He didn't know how much prison psychologists earned but Jennyviv had a wedding ring and she certainly seemed like a woman that would be married to a doctor or whatever who was minted.

When she turned in to a pair of gates he drove past and parked up on the road, gave her five minutes to take her coat off and then went up and rang the doorbell. The Saab was the only car on the drive.

When she opened the door he saw a look of alarm flit over her face followed by a professional mask that was distant and caring at the same time. She was all, 'Aidan, what are you doing here? You know this isn't allowed,' but her eyes were saying, 'He's a lot stronger than I am.'

It was obvious he wasn't going to get asked in, so Aidan

came straight out with it and told her he loved her, she was the one woman who had ever done anything for him and he thought about her all the time.

Her face relaxed slightly then. She came outside, pulled the door to after her and said, 'Oh, Aidan,' and looked at him like he'd shat himself but it was OK because she wasn't the one who had to clean it up.

So then he stood there by her grand front door while she explained to him why it couldn't happen and how she didn't think of him that way, he had got confused about the nature of their relationship.

'Nah,' said Aidan. 'I just fancy you and I thought I'd give it a shot.'

She opened her mouth to say something else, but then thought better of it. Then she made her face go all frowny-serious and said, 'You can't come here again, you know. And I'm afraid I have to report this to my, my boss and the prison and they will tell the probation service. It doesn't mean anything will happen, but I have to tell them.' There was a pause and then she said, 'It doesn't mean I'm not flattered.' And then he was scuffing his trainers against the step and turning to walk off when she said, 'I heard – about what happened with the fire.'

'Did you? What did you hear happened?'

'I mean, I heard there was a fire, and that you were, implicated, rightly or wrongly. I was sorry to hear about it.'

'I didn't do it,' he said. 'I fuckin dint.'

'I believe you,' said Jennyviv. Aidan stuck his hands in his pockets and walked off down the herringbone paving.

Jennyviv told the man from the probation service that she was really worried about Aidan. She hadn't felt in any danger.

Obviously the whole crush thing was just a cry for help.

The man from the probation service said, 'Well,' and left it hanging, to show he thought she was talking crap.

48

S EAN SHAW HAD been with the Royal Marines in Helmand Province, and now he was seeing out his service in Cyprus, shagging holiday-makers in Ayia Napa and crossing his fingers his name didn't come up for a drug test.

He had been awarded the Military Cross after an engagement where his patrol was hit by a roadside bomb, and he successfully defended the ones who were left as they evacuated the casualties. He would tell the tale, all reluctant, over a cocktail in some bar. When he got to the part where he picked up the injured boy and backed into the ruined school while scanning the skyline for the flash of the sniper's muzzle, he was already easing down the girl's knickers in his mind.

He didn't think about his kids in Doncaster. His girlfriend had got used to being a single mum while he was in Afghanistan, and when he came home she found it was hard to share the remote and put up with the rough sex. He had always been into it and she did her best, but it was hard to enjoy being tossed around when Corben and Jessica, who were such light sleepers anyway, were just the other side of the cardboard walls. So when he got his final posting – to Cyprus! – she refused to go. He'd thought she would jump at the chance. All that sunshine, jetskis, Jägerbombs. But Kelly said Corben was finally settled at school, Greek food gave her thrush, and incidentally when was he going to do something about those perished soffits?

So now here he was, on his tod. Some days Kelly texted him a photo of a painting one of the kids had done, and then he lay on his bunk brooding. He stored things up until he got leave and then went out looking for girls. Usually they would go to her hotel room or a quiet stretch of beach, and she would be pissed and so she would let him do whatever, and as he was pumping away he would think about pulling the trigger and seeing the top of the sniper's head burst like a paintball against the metal of the water tower, and that would really get him going. Once he gave this strawberry blonde Scouser a few slaps round the head as he came and made her ear bleed, so he stayed all night and then took her for lunch at this posh hotel, and although it cost him half a week's pay, it was worth it because she never said anything.

He told a journalist who turned up that he dreamed about the dead bodies and the injured boy, and after he had read it printed in a Sunday supplement he really started to have the dreams. It was weird as fuck because he had made some of the details up, but now they seemed real. He started to read up on Islamism and politics and thought about leaving the Marines to go and volunteer in Yemen or wherever as part of the global crusade.

When he heard about his cousin dying and how there was this Asian lad who had basically torched the place and got away with it because of the fucking liberal middle classes being so soft on the Muslims, he went white with rage. He suddenly saw his future more clearly than ever before. His place wasn't in the Middle East defending other people. It was in Britain defending his own family from the murderers.

Obviously he didn't say any of that to his CO. He just said he felt he had done his time in combat and wanted to start making the transition to a civilian future, and the CO was just relieved to be discharging a soldier who was happy and fully able and well-adjusted and wouldn't be popping up in *Panorama* documentaries saying Her Majesty's armed services had let him down.

49

ABOUT A MONTH after the inquest, there was a knock on the front door at five in the morning. It was just getting light. Jay was staying because he and Shana had had a row and she'd bogged off to her mum's again, and although an empty flat usually meant party time, there wasn't so much as a slice of bread in the place or a penny in Jay's pocket, so he had gone back to Jasmine's. When he was woken up by the knocking he went to the door in his jogging bottoms, and as soon as he opened it Bob Hardacre punched him in the face. It was only a glancing blow, but it still broke Jay's nose, and he stood there in the hall spitting blood and saying, 'What the fuck's the matter with you?'

Bob Hardacre rocked on his heels and stared back at him. His head was wobbling a bit from side to side, and his eyes were red like an alkie's. He was wearing suit trousers and a grubby T-shirt that said *Surf's Up!* on it, and his hair stuck out at all angles. He had a cricket bat in his hand and he was waggling it around like a baseball player waiting for the pitch. There was a smell of booze and sweat coming off him in waves.

'Where is he? Tell him to come down. I'll kill him. I'll knock his fucking head off,' he was saying, and more along those lines. His voice had gone all wonky too, and he looked like it would only take a couple of slaps and he'd be kneeling down on the grass wailing and wretching.

Jay looked at him dead-eyed from sleepiness or lack of pity.

'He's not here mate. He's moved away. They've had this big row. He's . . . gone to Bolton.' Which was a downright lie. Aidan was fast on upstairs, dreaming of a McChicken Sandwich and probably handling himself in his sleep.

But Bob Hardacre wasn't to know that. In fact he seemed relieved to hear that Aidan wasn't there, and he did actually slump down and sit on the garden wall and open his mouth to unburden his heart to Aidan's brother. But Jay had reached round behind the door and picked up the brass poker that Jasmine kept there, in case of burglars and rapists, and he waved it in Bob Hardacre's face and told him to fuck off and sort himself out, and if he turned up there again Jay would see to it Bob ended up face down in the Don.

Bob was so surprised he did as he was told. He shuffled off back through the estate and waited for a bus to take him back up to the barn conversion in Ringinglow where he and his wife were having their mental breakdowns.

When Aidan woke up and heard what had happened, he was livid. He kept going on about 'no one smacks my little brother,' and so on, but Jasmine told him to shut up and eat his cornflakes. She said it was all very well strutting about like a boxer, but not everyone who came to the door looking for him was going to crumble like Bob Hardacre. 'What are you going to do, take on all comers?'

'Aye,' said Jay. 'And one day they'll turn up with carving knives or a petrol bomb, and you and me mam'll be burned like toast.'

When they put it like that, Aidan quietened down a bit and said maybe he ought to move out for a bit so as not to bring any more shit on Jasmine.

Jasmine said, oh no, he wasn't fucking off again like last time so they wouldn't hardly see him for another five years.

But Jay said there was always the sofa at the flat. No one would know they were there because the flat was in Shana's name. It was studentsville up that end of town. No one knew them there. It would be a right laugh. And Shana would be fine with it. So Aidan packed some clothes and they set off. They called in to the camping shop to nick a sleeping bag on the way.

As it turned out, Shana wasn't all that fine with it after all. When she came back to the flat, on the Tuesday, with the pushchair and two big plastic bags full of nappies and all that, she saw Aidan lying on the sofa cutting his fingernails and said, cool as you like, 'Who the fuck are you?'

When Aidan had explained, she sent him off to put the kettle on, and by the time Jay got back from work she had taught him how to sterilise Kasey's bottle and change a nappy too. But later she took Jay into the bedroom to have a private word, which to judge from the shouting was, 'You don't want *her* getting hurt but what about Kasey? And *me*?' Then Jay's low voice saying they wouldn't find him here, they were safe. And so on. Then they came out and Shana gave Aidan a sweet but flimsy smile and they all ate packet rice with Dolmio on it for tea. Shana blanked Jay all evening but she didn't make Aidan leave, and at night when he was on the sofa and Kasey had finally stopped bawling he heard the pair of them humping and moaning in the bedroom, trying to make Kasey a little brother or sister.

In the morning Shana said she didn't want him being seen out and about, so he should stay in the flat and her and Jay could do the shopping and what have you.

'Like prison,' said Aidan, 'except at prison you get to stretch your legs every now and then.'

But Shana said take it or leave it, so he agreed.

The next day Jay and Shana were rowing again about the wrong size nappies, and then the next day about a text Shana got from some lad, and Aidan figured out that this is how it was with these two, shouting and raving one minute and the beast with two backs the next. And Shana seemed to like it when he made faces at Kasey and kept her entertained, so he settled in for a long stay. Every morning he stuffed his sleeping bag down behind the sofa and skinned up.

About once a week Jay and Shana would have a big row and she would trundle the pushchair down the corridor to the lift and stay at her mum's for a night or two, and then it would just be the brothers, playing on the Xbox and drinking cans, listening to music that was on way too fucking loud. Even though the flat was in Shana's name, it was like it was their flat and she was just a visitor.

'You want to keep your heads down a bit,' she said one day after the bloke downstairs had been banging on the ceiling about the noise. 'If the council evict us I'll just stay at me mam's, but you two'll be out on the street. See how you like that.'

'Piece of piss,' said Aidan, but that night and the night after they kept a lid on things.

At first it was a laugh being holed up in the flat. He would send Jay out for Rizlas and baccy, and as soon as he walked in the door Aidan would say, 'Don't take your coat off. We've run out of milk.' Aidan thought this was pretty funny, but Jay started to get cheesed off, and one day when Aidan sent him out to Lidl for a bottle of brandy, he got on the tram instead and spent a few hours knocking around Meadowhall, then met up with this girl he knew who worked behind the bar at the bowling alley. They ended up at her place out in Rawmarsh, and the next morning when he finally waltzed in smelling of a girl's bed, Aidan had a face like thunder. But Jay just plonked a half-bottle down on the table and said, 'There you go bruv. Weren't waiting on it specially were you?'

After that the fun started to go out of being stuck in the flat, and as the weeks went by Aidan seemed to get more and more stir crazy. Sitting inside on his arse all day didn't do much for his health. He got podgier and podgier and his skin turned greasy and started to get these flaky spots. His eyes seemed to get smaller and set back further in his head surrounded by these dark shadows. But more to the point he got this slack look in his face and seemed to be sinking into a trough of self-pity. He would sit with the telly on all day watching adverts for loans and personal injury lawyers. The low point was when Jay walked in on him wanking on the sofa in front of Lorraine Kelly.

'Fucking hell man,' he said, 'I have to sit there,' but although Aidan put himself away and wouldn't catch his eye, he didn't exactly seem ashamed. It was like all the shame had been sapped out of him.

'I have to get out of this chuffing flat,' he said while Jay was eating his Weetabix the next morning. 'I'm going off my sodding nut.'

'You've never been on it,' said Jay, and carried on eating. But then he put down his spoon and said, 'Fine. Just try not to attract attention, will you. If this place gets trashed Shana'll kill us. Her knickers are tight shut at the best of times.'

'Is that why you've been on with that bird from Rawmarsh?' said Aidan, but Jay didn't say anything to that. He just picked up his keys and left, leaving his bowl on the table next to yesterday's and the day before's.

After *Homes Under the Hammer* had finished Aidan pulled on his Nikes and strolled up to West Street. The sun was out, so he bought some cider and sat on Devonshire Green drinking and watching the dudes in the skatepark. The next thing was, someone was being chucked out of the bar at the Forum, and when Aidan wandered over he saw it was Mark Crabbe.

'Hey up, Mark,' said Aidan. 'Where's Shelley?'

'Alright,' said Mark. 'She's in there. She chucked up over one of the tables and now she's barricaded herself in the bogs.'

It was half past eleven in the morning, and you could see how that wouldn't go down well with the management. The two of them stood there watching the entrance to the Forum from across the road, Aidan swigging on his cider and Mark doing his best to stand up straight. He must have been out all night. His head was wobbly and he kept licking his lips. The bar manager who had chucked him out was standing in the doorway looking back at them, trying to look hard in his black shirt and trousers combo.

There was a commotion behind him in the bar, and then Shelley appeared with two more bar staff, a man and a woman, holding an arm each behind her back. She was snarling and twisting, but they had good momentum and managed to get her through the doorway and then sling her out into the road. She stood there effing and blinding back at them till a blue Micra pipped its horn at her to get out of the way. She turned and gave it the rods and shouted at the Micra driver to fuck off, and then turned and gave the same to the Forum staff again, and then came over to the other side where Aidan and Mark Crabbe were standing.

'What the fuck do you want?' she said to Aidan.

'Here,' said Aidan, and passed her a can.

'I should fucking stab you, after last time,' she said.

'Yeah, well,' said Aidan, and the three of them walked over to Devonshire Green to where Aidan had been sitting. Mark got out a bag of pills and they took a couple each, and the day went downhill from there.

The next morning Jay was in a right temper. Apparently Shelley Turner had lamped a traffic warden and ended up having to be pepper sprayed, and Mark Crabbe had tried to stop the police car driving off with her and had his foot run over and broken in three places. The only bright spot was that there would have to be an investigation by the IPCC, and that meant a load of extra paperwork and hassle for the plod. Aidan had been there cheering the pair of them on, stripped to the waist and holding a pizza box.

Jay said, 'I thought you were going to keep a low profile.'

But Aidan just lifted a buttock and farted. 'Soz,' he said.

After that he went out most days, not getting ratted but just slorming himself round the streets, getting a break from the telly and the stale air of the flat. It seemed to be doing him some good. He got back into showering again, knocked the weed on the head and even picked up a bit of cash in hand with a builder who was renovating this house in Sharrowvale. It had been infested with students for years, and now some GP had bought it and was having it gutted and done up again proper nice. Aidan got all the grunt work, shifting rubble, lifting joists and so on. There was a little river out the back and he would stand on the wall and piss into it every morning after his sausage and egg breadcake.

'Jesus,' said Neil the plasterer one day, smoking a fag. 'Your piss is like gravy.'

Aidan wasn't bothered. But he looked up and saw Neil wasn't the only one watching. There was a face in the window of the house next door. When he looked up, it disappeared.

When Aidan finished for the day, there was this woman hanging around, and as he came out of the door she came straight up to him. He was ready for a bollocking for flashing his cock, but it turned out she was a nurse.

'You need to get yourself down the doctor's,' she said. 'That could be cirrhosis, kidney damage, or owt.'

He said, 'Nah.'

But she said she was serious, and she started going on about all these awful conditions that brown piss could be a symptom of. So in the end he promised he would make an appointment with the GP.

The nurse was there again the next day, and of course Aidan hadn't done fuck-all about getting an appointment, so she scolded him in a friendly way and they got talking. She was called Liz and although she was reasonably fit and not that much older than Aidan, he didn't fancy her. She used to bring him a mug of tea and they would sit on the steps and talk about the train wrecks that were their lives. The other lads on site teased him about spending his break nattering to her, but he didn't care.

Liz had spent her twenties and thirties living with a guy who said he didn't want kids and then of course he had left her for a blonde postgraduate student and sprogged off inside eighteen months.

'It isn't too late,' said Aidan, trying to be nice, 'If you met someone . . .'

'I'd have to meet someone first,' said Liz. 'Anyway . . .' She made a face, like, 'leave it,' so he did.

It was good to have someone to talk to who wasn't a builder or a knob, a girlfriend, a mam or a brother or sister, a solicitor, a custody sergeant, a bailiff, a dealer, a fence or a tramp. Liz sorted him an appointment to go and see someone about his dark-coloured piss, and he bought her a Chinese and some cans to say thanks.

50

J AY SAID SHANA was nervous about Aidan going out all the time, in case he got recognised. But Aidan told him to relax.

'No one's going to do anything,' he said. 'That old guy was a one-off. They'll all have calmed down by now, and anyway, none of it was my fault and they know it.'

When that got back to Shana she said, in that case, why didn't he piss off back to Jasmine's? But that was just the sort of shit people said. She wasn't really bothered about him being there. For one thing, she and little Kasey were hardly there themselves. Her mum's bipolar was playing up and she didn't like leaving her on her tod. Her stepdad Kevin was on medication himself. Half the time he was asleep and the other half he was sitting at the kitchen table mulling over what had happened to his kid sister, even though that was years ago and anyone could have bad luck. Meanwhile Shana's mum was on the sofa in the other room with the telly blaring, thinking she was fat and why not end it all, with bowls and chip papers stacking up around her. So Shana reckoned it was a good idea to be around to keep an eye on things. When she put Kasey on the carpet and turned the telly on mute, a bit of light came into her mum's eyes, and that could only be a good thing. The trouble was, her mum had started saying that mad shit from before about the shadow people and CCTV surveillance. It was just her mum going on, but she didn't like to leave Kasey with her. They said mentally ill people were no more dangerous than anyone else, but you never knew.

It was all a bit exhausting, and the last thing she wanted to be bothered with was Jay's knobhead older brother.

Jay said not to worry about it anyway, because Aidan had got some regular work and seemed to be spending half his time slurping tea with this nurse.

Shana said, Christ, she'd heard about nurses, that dirty bugger better not be turning the flat into a knocking shop.

But Jay said, no, it wasn't like that: this nurse was, like, forty and she was more likely to dose Aidan up with camomile tea than to jump into the sack with him. 'She's a calming influence,' he said.

Shana said, 'Yeah, right,' and rolled her eyes, but she left it at that.

The truth was that Jay was dead happy when Shana was fretting over Aidan, because it kept the heat off him. The week before, Danni from Rawmarsh had told him she had morning sickness, and since she was a Catholic there was no way she was getting rid of it.

He had sat fiddling with the salt cellar in Nando's not knowing what to say. He was half sconned out because of how Shana would hit the roof and half dead pleased with himself for having done the deed. Danni had black hair and a slim body and didn't give him earache over nappies and Sudocrem, and even though that was all to come, just now she looked like the better option. So they went back to hers and got with it, and lying there afterwards Jay made all sorts of promises which he couldn't keep without breaking the promises he had already made to Shana.

Danni played it cool and that got Jay all the more hooked.

She was dead confident and had the look of someone who might get through to the second round on *X Factor*. It was like when the baby came she would still have clean hair and dealing with nappies would just be like doing her nails, something she did off to one side without you hardly noticing. But you could tell she was off her nut on hormones because she cried watching *Dog the Bounty Hunter* and came back from Morrisons with two bags of celery. She showed Jay how you could dunk it in mayonnaise, and Jay was like, 'This will always be our food,' but in the back of his mind he was thinking that he had said the same thing to Shana about chicken jalfrezi.

After that it was a mad juggling act, trying to do right by Kasey and keep Shana off his back and make sure Danni was okay, all at the same time. When he was with Shana and Kasey it was really good, and he was angry at himself for messing it all up just for a bit on the side. He told Shana he loved her, and kept making up his mind to tell Danni, sorry, it was over, and if she had the kid anyway he would just have to live with it but he wouldn't be a hands-on dad. Then he and Shana would have one of their rows or she would go back to check on her mum, and five minutes after she left he would be thinking of Danni and her tight little arse and he would find himself thumbing out a saucy message on his phone.

Every day he walked past Mothercare on his way to work and he saw the prams in the window in front of massive photos of babies laughing and he thought to himself what a fucking mess it all was. It all went round and round in his head, and he felt sick and tried to remember what it was he used to get excited about when he was at college looking forward to his life.

Then one day he had a brainfart and called Shana 'Danni'

when he came inside her, and although he explained it away, after that she had her bullshit radar on at maximum strength. She kept texting every five minutes and quizzing him about where he was and who he was with, and once he found her going through his Facebook. Luckily he secretly had WhatsApp but you couldn't see it on the home screen, and that was how he got in touch with Danni. But Danni was getting fidgety as well, asking him when was he going to tell his ex he was having another kid and when was he going to kick her out of his flat, and wasn't it weird sharing a flat with his ex and his brother?

One day Jay called in for a quick one at this pub, putting off going home and having to deal with everything. An old mate of Nick's called Carl was there, and he came over to say hi. Carl said to pass on a message to Aidan that he had seen a lad called Dave who said that this girl Suzie they used to know had died. Jay said he would.

Jay went home and when Aidan came home he passed on the message.

Aidan started with these questions. How did Carl seem, like he was taking the piss or for real? How did he know? When did it happen? What had Suzie died of? And when Jay shrugged and said he didn't know, Aidan started bouncing off the walls and grinding his teeth like the old days. But Jay's phone was going off with messages from Danni and texts from Shana, both asking to him to call, so he just told Aidan to chill out and was relieved when he put his jacket on and stormed off out the flat, slamming the door, and Jay could concentrate on staring at the floor feeling sorry for himself.

51

AIDAN TURNED UP at Liz's house about half-past
six.

'Hey up,' she said carefully. He might come round after
work but after he had gone he didn't usually come back. 'You
alright, mate?'

But obviously he wasn't. She stood aside and let him steam
down the hall and rattle around the kitchen while she put the
kettle on and made sure she had an escape route if things got
ugly. Not that it seemed likely. He was dead het up, but not
angry, exactly. He was going on about some girl, Suzie, and
how she had tried to top herself but failed, or maybe she had
managed it. Someone called Carl was a fucking liar, and Jay,
who was Aidan's brother, was acting like a dick.

He was all red in the face and hyperventilating, and for a
minute she thought it might be the beginning of a seizure. But
then she got him to sit down and regulate his breathing, and
stood rubbing his neck while he got himself under control.
It was the first time they had touched each other intimate-
ly and although they were just mates and anyway it wasn't
exactly a sexual situation, she was struck by how big he was,
the thick muscles in his neck and so on, and in an instant
she saw him in a different light. Not worse or better, just
different.

When he had calmed down she put a couple of mugs of
tea on the table and managed to get the story out of him,

about Suzie being his ex and a junkie and how he had messed thing up.

'Sounds like you both did,' said Liz.

And then he said how Suzie had made the suicide attempt and he had left.

Liz raised her eyebrows at that.

Aidan said, 'Her brother thought it was best and so did I.'

He looked ashamed but Liz didn't say anything for a minute, and then she said, 'So now this Carl says she's dead?'

He nodded.

'And your little brother's involved how?' Aidan made an irritated face and waved his hand, so she waited again and then said, 'So now she's dead and you think this time she managed it?'

He rubbed his hands over his face and then back over his hair. 'Yeah. I don't know. What does it matter? She's dead.'

It was hard to argue with that so Liz put her tea down and stood up, and gave him a hug.

Aidan said he had to go to Swansea to see about Suzie.

Liz said, 'The funeral?'

He said he hadn't thought that far. He didn't even know if it was true, because this Carl seemed to suddenly have it in for him, and even if it was, it could have happened ages ago. Like, months.

But he was determined to go. Liz looked up the train and bus times, but it was such a long way to Swansea that there was no way of getting there that night. Aidan said he would go in the morning, but he showed no signs of leaving, so Liz made him up the spare bed and cooked them a chilli con carne for tea.

She got up at five for her shift and caught him for a quick hello as he was leaving. The poor bastard didn't even have a coat. She gave him thirty quid.

She said, 'Soz, it's all I've got. Bit short this month. What about work?' He looked at her, and she said, 'Want me to call in and say you've had a bereavement?' and he nodded. So after he had gone she wrote a note and stuck it through the letterbox of the house they were renovating, and jumped on the bus for the Northern General and a pig of a day treating kids who had tipped up pans of boiling water, RTCs, violent drunks and all the usual.

52

AIDAN MADE HIS way to Swansea on the National Express. He sat staring out at the motorway as it zipped past, biting his nails and feeling carsick. At Worcester he got off and bought some cans, and then again when he changed coaches at Cardiff.

He went to Suzie's house and looked through the lounge window at her stepdad Steve sitting in his wheelchair looking knackered as fuck but alive, at least. Aidan was going to go in and see him but Suzie's brother Billy headed him off at the door.

'No you don't,' he said, fronting up. Then Steve called through, 'Who is it?' and Billy looked uncertainly over his shoulder, came out of the house and pulled the door to, and walked Aidan round the side of the house.

He said Aidan shouldn't have come, he was just a skidmark who had been one of the shits that Suzie had met on her way down the toilet, and if he came back again Billy would kill him. Aidan sized him up then with a smirk, but Billy said he might look weak as shit but he could stick a knife in Aidan easy as, and he would too, it didn't mean fuck-all to him. Then he seemed to back down a bit, and told Aidan some of the details so he would go away.

Apparently Suzie had been off the gear again for a while but had got back into it in a big way a few months back. She had fallen in with this arsehole called Creasey who had knocked her about – bruises and cracked ribs and fag burns and missing teeth and so on – and he had kept hold of the smack and doled it out in instalments to keep her under his thumb. Then Creasey had been convicted for burglary and got six weeks inside, so Billy and Steve had been round there trying to convince Suzie to up sticks. She was full of talk like junkies always were, saying she was going to do it and move away, to Sheffield maybe, and they knew what she meant by that, and how she was going into rehab again. But she kept getting hold of the gear and finding excuses not to leave, and then one day she lobbed a whisky bottle at Steve and it smashed on the arm of his wheelchair and showered him in broken glass. Things had gone from bad to worse and when Creasey got out, some busybody in the flat next door told him about all the comings and goings, and he tret Suzie worse than ever. First she couldn't speak properly because of this split lip, and then she was holding her arm close up against her stomach for three days till Billy took her down the Morriston to get it put in a sling. She was so drunk that the sour-faced sister made her sit on a trolley for five hours till she sobered up and they could treat her 'without fear of verbal or physical abuse.' After they had patched her up and Billy took her home, Creasey broke his nose and said if he came round again then he would drown Suzie in the bath and make it look like an accident.

Steve wanted to call the police, but Billy said, 'What's the fucking point? She'll just deny everything and after they've gone she'll get another kicking.' So they left her alone for a couple of weeks, and the next thing they knew the neighbour told them there was an ambulance down Suzie's road. She had overdosed on the smack, and no one would ever know if it was an accident or her only escape.

Aidan bent over and leant his head on the garden fence and cried. 'And well you might,' said Billy. 'It's because of cunts like you she's dead.' There was an old woman pulling a Burberry shopping trolley down the pavement, but she didn't bat an eyelid. Shit like this happened all the time round that way.

Billy said that Bethan who Aidan had shacked up with was still around, fat as hell and washed up with kids by different fathers. 'One of them's probably yours,' he said, maybe hoping to get a rise out of Aidan, but Aidan just said, 'Where can I find this Creasey?'

Billy said, 'Fuck's sake man, what's the point?'

They stood there for a bit longer and in the end Billy gave Aidan an address just to get rid of him.

'Don't come back here,' he said, 'I don't want my dad to see you,' and he went back inside.

It took ages to find the address, mainly because Aidan was still half pissed from the cans and his phone was dead so he had to go around asking folk, and most of them walked off without making eye contact as soon as he approached, thinking he was asking them for money. But in the end he found the road, a cul-de-sac on the edge of an estate. At the end of the road there was an entrance to some woods with a load of fly-tipping. Aidan stood in the rain and looked at it, just household rubbish and toilet seats and kitchen unit carcasses. Further in to the woods there were plenty of squashed beer cans and fag packets and burger wrappers, with the odd needle and used condom chucked in.

He went into the woods and doubled back behind the houses, and worked out which was Creasey's number. Then he kicked down the bit of rotten fence and went into the back yard, picked up a lump of breeze block that was holding the plastic patio table down and hoyed it through the kitchen window.

A face appeared at an upstairs window and then there was a gap of a few seconds before this dude flung open the back door looking right pissed off. He had on some trackie bottoms and nothing else, and he was dripping wet. He had a baseball bat in his hand.

'Didn't get you out the bath, did I?' said Aidan, but this guy, who must be Creasey, didn't stop to chat. He came out swinging a big forehand, and Aidan had to dodge his head backwards to avoid getting a broken skull.

As soon as Creasey had brought the bat back the other way, Aidan leapt forward and stamped his work boot on the top of his bare foot. You could hear the snapping of all those little bones. Creasey made a pasty shocked face and stood still long enough for Aidan to punch him hard in the guts three times. Then Creasey started to fold in half and Aidan switched his attention to his face. There was a spray of blood as his head whipped back, and he fell heavily on to the doorstep. Without pausing Aidan stepped over him and kicked him a good few times in the nuts and then in the head, till the adrenalin was starting to run out and Creasey had stopped squirming. He was just sort of laid there curled up like a pickled cockle, with a tiny rattling noise as if he was trying to breath but there was blood or something in his windpipe getting in the way.

Aidan stepped back and half turned to go. But then he saw another breeze block in the corner of the yard, picked it up, took it over to where Creasey was lying and wanged it down as hard as he could on to Creasey's head.

The tiny breathing noise stopped. A lot of blood started to appear under Creasey's head and ooze out over the doorstep.

Aidan walked back out through the wood and walked into the city centre as fast as he could and caught the National Express home.

53

ON THE WAY back he managed to borrow a charger off this prim blonde student. He was a bit pop-eyed after what had gone on, jiggling in his seat and looking round at the other passengers as if they might morph into policemen. So when he asked the girl for the charger she obviously felt like she couldn't say no.

Once he had a bit of charge, the texts started coming in. One from Jay and one from Shana, and then three or four from Jasmine saying 'Were r u' and so on. So he called Shana who said there was something the matter with Jay but she didn't know what. He had texted something about this hard man turning up and banging on the flat door looking for Aidan. She had tried ringing but it went straight to answerphone.

So then he gave Danni a call, but that went to answerphone too. He couldn't be arsed ringing Jasmine and getting a load of grief so he sat playing Sniper 3D Assassin. As the coach pulled in to Nottingham bus station, the student kept glancing at him, and only when the coach had pulled in to the bay did she stand up and asked him for the charger back. She got a rucksack down off the overhead rack and stood there. Aidan unplugged the charger, gave it her back and said thanks with a nice smile, and she gave him a quick unfriendly smile and got off.

On the way to Mansfield Danni rang back, but there was hardly any signal and all Aidan could get was that she was at the hospital. So then he did ring Jasmine but it rang out and rang out every time he tried.

It was dark by the time he got into Sheffield. He caught a tram up through town and walked up to Hanover, under the underpass and up to hide in the bushes and see what was going on. It was all quiet, but there was a police van parked up and part of the area around the tower was taped off. He went back down to West Street and got on a bus to the Northern General.

Jasmine finally rang back while he was on the bus. It was hard to make out what had happened because she was ranting and raving – calling Aidan a fucking bastard and so on, so he guessed it had something to do with him – and then sobbing and going on about Jay like he was a little kid. But the long and short of it was that Jay had come off the balcony of the flat on to the concrete below and now he was in surgery and probably wouldn't survive the night.

When he got there, there were Jasmine and Danni both with their eye-liner smeared by crying, and Danni's cheek was red raw. Her bulge was really showing now and Jasmine kept looking sideways at her and going, 'Oh my God.' It was like the fact Jay had got Danni up the duff was as big a shock to her as him falling off the balcony, but then again the two of them had never met until that day.

Aidan drank a can of Monster Energy and got the story out of them.

Apparently about two in the afternoon Jay had texted Shana and Danni these messages about a bloke trying to get in the flat, and then his phone had gone dead. Shana's mum had been agitated and scared to come downstairs 'because of the removal men', so she didn't want to leave her. That was when she sent the text to Aidan and also one to Jasmine, and then she figured Jay was a big boy and could look after himself.

But Jay's text had really shit Danni up. It was all those hormones. She jumped in her mum's 208 and pegged it down through Meadowhall and Attercliffe in eighteen minutes. When she got there the flat door was wide open, and there was no one inside, but the sofa was tipped over and the floor was strewn with smashed bottles and takeaway boxes. The balcony door was open and she went out and looked down and saw Jay lying there at the bottom all folded up and bleeding.

She said, 'I don't know how long he was laid there, but no cunt had called an ambulance or nothing. Like you wouldn't notice if a lad falls off a fucking balcony in broad daylight.' Aidan was holding on to the Monster Energy can as if it was a lifebelt, and looking like he might deal out a pasting to the vending machine.

Danni rang for the ambulance and the police as she ran downstairs. Jay was lying there unconscious but he still seemed to be breathing. The operator kept her on the line asking questions like, 'Are his airways free?' and 'Is there anyone there with first aid experience?' but all she could do was keep saying, 'I don't know,' and running her hand over her face and looking around for someone to help but it was a quiet corner by the bushes and there was only an old lady who looked across from the walkway and kept going.

She wasn't allowed to go with Jay in the ambulance. They said sorry, but there wouldn't be room because of the seriousness of his injuries. She thought from the looks on their faces that they didn't want her in there in case he died on the way. So even though she was pregnant and in a right state, she had to drive to the Northern General in the 208. But first she rang Jasmine and introduced herself and gave her the bad news, and then Jasmine rang Shana.

At the hospital it was a madhouse. They were busy as fuck anyway, and then there were police swirling around because of the circumstances. Jasmine said the police weren't ruling anything out at this stage, meaning it could have been attempted murder or an accident or he could have chucked himself off. 'Did he fuck,' said Danni. 'He had everything to live for.'

That was right after Shana had arrived, and she was all, 'Who the fuck are you?' and Danni gave her a disdainful look that made it bleeding obvious, and the next minute they were screeching and swearing at each other and Shana gave Danni a big hard slap on the side of the face and stormed off sobbing for a fag by the entrance. Jasmine went out to see if she was alright, but Shana said the cheating bastard got what was coming to him and he could die for all she cared, and then she left. So Jasmine came back inside, and while they were waiting for news she started getting to know Danni, seeing as, even though the circumstances weren't ideal, she was carrying her new grandchild.

'Yeah,' said Aidan, 'but what about this cunt banging on the door?'

54

DANNI SAID SHE didn't know eff all about that, just what Jay had said in his text.

'And what *did* he say?' said Aidan.

She said she didn't know, just that there was this bloke. Then Aidan kept going on about 'what, exactly?' and she kept saying, 'I don't know,' till he made her get her phone out and read it to him.

'Mad bloke tryin to get in flat gonna lamp him in a minute.'

Aidan said he would go back to Hanover and see if the neighbours saw anything, but Jasmine said that was a waste of time. No one would talk to him because he would scare them shitless and he would end up getting arrested for smashing windows or something, knowing him.

Aidan said, OK, what would she suggest? And Jasmine was quiet for a moment, deciding, and then she said that Shawsy's cousin was out of the Army now and Vicky Shaw was putting it about that Aidan was going to get his comeuppance. 'This Sean's a right toughie apparently. Killed twenty Talibans in one day, and all that. He'll be the one what's done it.'

So then Aidan did trash the vending machine, except it was built to last: he punched and kicked at the glass, but it didn't break, so then he started rocking it back and forth until it toppled over with a crash that reverberated up and down the corridor. 'Fuck's sake,' said Danni. People were looking at them and there was the echo of security men running down the corridor, so Aidan stuck his hands in his pockets and made his way off at pace.

It was night now, and there were plenty of people out for their Saturday night drink. He walked along Herries Road towards Hillsborough, without thinking much about where he was going. After a while he looked up and the Polish car wash was suddenly there in front of him. It was shut but there was a light on in the flat-roofed office. Maybe they left a light on to put off thieves.

It was like a sign. He thought about Nick and how they had never paid that bastard Karol back, and now he would. He doubled back to the petrol station and bought a plastic jerrycan and filled it up. While he was queuing up to pay he could see himself on the CCTV monitor in the corner with the date and time printed across the bottom.

At the car wash he got in behind the office where he couldn't be seen, took off one shoe and then the sock, and put the shoe back on. It was cold on his naked foot. He unscrewed the cap of the jerrycan and stuffed the sock inside to soak it in petrol. Then he pulled it back out so it was dangling out the top, took out his lighter and tried to light it. At first it wouldn't go – and then it caught suddenly and flames were licking round his hands. He lobbed the jerrycan at the office door, turned and as he ran heard it go up with a *whumf.* The petrol on his hands had gone out but they were hurting to fuck. He didn't stop running.

As it happened the office wasn't empty. Lisa, Connor's old flame, was in there with Sebastian. When the petrol bomb went up they fair shit themselves. Sebastian yanked himself out and they ran around in a blind panic, pulling on their clothes and looking for a way out. There were flames coming through the letterbox so Sebastian put a chair through the window and they climbed out. Lisa cut her foot pretty badly on the glass.

Later some people said this was the worst thing Aidan did, trying to burn two love birds to death out of sheer jealousy. But Irene from the taxi place said how was he to know they were at it in there, it wasn't a brothel, and probably those Eastern Europeans had paid him to torch the place for the insurance. Irene had been down on Aidan all his life, and now when it had finally all kicked off she was suddenly his biggest fan. She wasn't the only one. All over Facebook people were posting links to the news story saying he was a fucking ledge.

Aidan ran up the road to the snooker club he used to go to. He played a quick frame to calm his nerves and then rang round some mates to find out Vicky Shaw's address. Apparently she lived at the top end of Foxhill, up towards Grenoside. He memorised the road and house number.

By this time it was half past ten at night. He took the thick end of a cue from the rack, left the club and walked up through the estate to the house his mate had said. He went into the front garden and looked in through the front window, and there was Vicky Shaw and her fella and that scrote Bartholomew, all spragged out on the three-piece suite with their eyes glued to some action film on this enormous telly.

Aidan tried the front door and the daft bastards hadn't even locked it, so he walked straight down the hall and in to where they were sitting and whacked Bartholomew round the side of the head with the snooker cue. Bartholomew slipped forward on to his knees and didn't pass out exactly but just stayed there with his hands on his head not moving or saying anything, with blood trickling between his fingers and down his hands.

Vicky Shaw's fella sat looking up at Aidan white as a ghost. Then he made to get up but Aidan brandished the cue at him and he stayed sitting.

Aidan opened his mouth to speak to Vicky but at that moment she screamed, so he punched her in the face with his free hand and she sprawled backwards on the sofa. This time her fella did get up so Aidan punched him too, hard. His nose burst and he fell back and knocked the telly over and lay there, and suddenly the noise of the action film stopped and the house was totally quiet.

Vicky was sitting on the sofa glaring at Aidan and he was glaring at her. Then a voice wavered out, 'Mummy!' from the stairs. Vicky put her hand up to stop the blood dribbling into her mouth and called out, 'Go back to bed love, it's alright,' and they waited, but the voice didn't say anything else and no one appeared in the doorway.

'Where is he?' said Aidan, and of course Vicky said, 'What the fuck are you talking about?'

Aidan threatened her with the cue, but she just looked daggers at him. So he turned to the other two. Bartholomew had kind of slumped over, still holding his head with more and more blood running down his hands and wrists and on to the sleeves of his top. Vicky's fella was sparko on the carpet, with the massive telly half on top of him. Aidan went and stood over him and raised the cue above his head and looked at Vicky.

She said, 'He's not here, alright?' And then, 'I've said he's fucking not here. I dunno where he is. Look just fucking get out, alright?'

Aidan lowered the cue and jabbed his thumb towards the ceiling. 'Shall I go upstairs?' he said.

She went white as a sheet and shook her head.

'Where is he then?'

She gave him an address, but Aidan said he wasn't born yesterday, it could be any old crap she was giving him. Then he told her to ring him up, so she got her phone out and found the number.

'What's his name?' he asked as she passed him the phone, and she told him.

Sean answered and Aidan said, 'Hey up Sean, it's Aidan Wilson here, I'm at your Vicky's. I think you'd better get down here.'

55

'**Y**OU BETTER FUCK off out of it now,' said Vicky once he had hung up. 'He'll be straight on to the pigs now. You've probably got about ten minutes.'

'Be serious,' said Aidan. 'He ant chucked my brother off a tower block just to go grassing me up. What'll they do me for, anyway? Common assault?'

Bartholomew was slowly crumpling up by the easy chair and his blood was getting worked into the carpet as he writhed around. It didn't look like a common assault charge. Vicky's fella was still lying under the telly, but his eyes were darting from side to side and the telly was shifting slightly as he moved.

'Fucking get up, Paul,' said Vicky, all irritated. You could tell she was cheesed off with having to settle for a wet sausage roll like him. But you had to be realistic when you were in your thirties with gland trouble and a couple of kids in tow.

Paul slowly slid the broken telly off him and sat up into a crouch, watching Aidan the whole time. He crept over to the sofa and sat down by Vicky. Aidan turned and walked out of the room. They heard him go up the hall, slip the latch and put the chain on the door, then come back down and past the open doorway into the kitchen. He came back with a big pair of scissors in his hand, went straight up to Vicky and grabbed her by the hair. She was pulled forwards off the sofa on to her knees.

Paul was sat there fucking terrified, like most people would be in that situation.

Vicky was cursing and spitting, but Aidan held the silver scissors right in front of her face, like all it would take would be a sudden jab and he'd take an eye out, and she stopped struggling. Then he went at her hair with the scissors, hacking away so that long strands were falling off. Whenever she started struggling again, he poked at her scalp with the pointy end of the scissors and she flinched away and held her head still again. All this time Paul was sat watching with a face like he'd shat himself, and Bartholomew was dropping further and further out of consciousness on the floor by the gas fire. Every now and then one of his feet would scrape on the carpet and then go still again, like he was in so much pain he wanted to thrash about but his brain wasn't with it enough to make it happen. '

After a while Vicky had lost almost all of her hair except for one clump on the top that Aidan was holding her by. The rest was only tufts flecked with red where the scissors had jabbed her. She hadn't done any sobbing but her cheeks were wet where her tears had run down. She was still kneeling there in front of Aidan when her kids came downstairs again.

There was a girl and a boy, probably about eleven and nine. The boy stood there in his Spiderman pyjamas and stared. The girl had on flowery bottoms and a T-shirt. She said, 'Mam?'

'Shit,' said Paul.

'Go back to bed sweetheart,' said Vicky in a voice that was meant to sound reassuring but wasn't.

Aidan said, 'No.'

The kids stood there, still staring at their mother kneeling on the floor crying and surrounded by her own hair.

'What's your names?' said Aidan.

The boy said nothing. The girl said, 'I'm Candice, he's Adam.'

Aidan said, 'Hello Candice.'

Vicky said, 'No, no, no,' and started struggling.

Aidan let go of her hair and punched her in the face with the handle end of the scissors. 'Jesus,' he said. 'What do you take me for?' Vicky fell back against the foot of the sofa with blood streaming from her lip. Paul got down on his knees and held her, and she did start crying properly now, an I-can't-take-it wave of sobbing that set the children off too. Paul beckoned to them and they ran over so that the whole family was cuddled up in a terrified heap amongst the empty beercans.

When the whole story got out afterwards it was the haircutting that people said proved Aidan was a mad bastard. Even the people who thought he was a legend for giving two fingers to the police like that had to admit that cutting off a lass's hair with her kids stood watching was a pretty sick thing to do. Some people even said that if he had dragged her upstairs and had his way with her it would have been less pervy than what he did do. But anyone could have an opinion, and no one's opinion mattered except God's, and He didn't exist.

About this time it came on the news that a man from Sheffield was wanted in connection with an incident in Swansea in which another man had died. They showed a grainy picture of Aidan getting on the coach at Swansea bus station. Jasmine saw it on the telly in the relatives room at the hospital and bust into tears so Danni had to cuddle her head on her lap, with her ear resting against the bump. It was the icing on the cake. Danni thought, 'Piggin hell, what've I got me sen into?' but she didn't say owt. Then after Jasmine had sobbed for like fifteen minutes Danni couldn't take it. She made Jasmine sit up and went to stand outside the sliding doors until someone offered her a cigarette.

That was where she met Gavin, and, much later, she and Gavin got together, moved to Pontefract and set up a business installing wood burning stoves, and Gavin was a great dad to all their kids even though the first one wasn't his.

56

S EAN SHAW CAN'T have been far away because it was
no more than fifteen minutes between Aidan hanging up
and him hammering at the door like a jealous husband.

The kids were sat there with wide eyes and their arms
flung round Vicky, who looked like a scarecrow or someone
suffering from a dreadful illness. When the hammering started
her face jolted up but otherwise she didn't move a muscle. Her
fella Paul started to get up but Aidan had the half a snooker
cue in his hand again, and he just raised it a little and Paul
settled back down on the carpet with his arms round Vicky
and the kids. Bartholomew was out of it. So they all just
stayed where they were, the family cowering by the sofa and
Aidan standing over them in the middle of the room, while
Vicky's cousin banged on the door and yelled blue murder on
the path outside. He was so angry that it was hardly swearwords or even words at all – just mad raving. The lads in the
house opposite filmed him and uploaded it to YouTube as
GOING BERSERK!!! and got two hundred and thirty-seven
views before they had to take it down because of what happened afterwards.

After a minute or so Sean got fed up of squawking and
put his foot to the door. The first kick broke the latch and the
second one broke the chain. He stormed up the passage with
Afghanistan going off in his head again. There was even the
crackle of his radio headset. But he wasn't holding an assault

rifle. It was a black and yellow Stanley hammer just like the ones you can get in Homebase.

He arrived at the door to the living room, clocked Vicky and the rest of them in their weepy huddle and moved on Aidan without pausing for a second. At the same moment he swung the hammer, Aidan jabbed the half a cue right in his face. The brass thread where the other half screwed on tore straight through his lip, knocked out two teeth and gashed right into the roof of his mouth. Meanwhile the hammer connected with the point of Aidan's elbow. There was a smash of bone and the cue dropped out of his hand.

They stood there for a moment, Sean with blood pouring out of his gob like a woman's waters breaking, Aidan with his arm flopping about in all directions.

That Paul, Vicky's fella, chucked up. He caught most of it in his mouth but a bit spilled out.

The next second Sean Shaw was swinging the hammer again, but Aidan caught his arm with his free hand and planted his head right in Sean's face. Then they were toppling over and rolling all round the floor, belting each other with hands, feet, knees and so on, trying to get in a good bite or put out the other one's eye. Sean dropped the hammer. It was the most vicious fight you ever saw in your life, but useless too because they were both already so badly hurt. It was a bit like watching two bull sea lions gouging lumps out of one another on the rocks off Argentina, except instead of David Attenborough watching from a safe distance there was Bartholomew slumped there losing his vital signs in a pair of bloodstained Pumas.

While they were going at it, Vicky gestured at Paul with her eyes towards the hammer which was lying under Sean Shaw's thigh, as if to say, 'Pick that up and whack Aidan on the head with it and you'll be the big hero.' Paul did stand up, but then instead of the hammer he picked up Candice and Adam one in each arm, carried them into the hall and ran out through the broken doorway. He left the kids on the pavement and ran back up to the house going, 'Vix! Come on Vix!' in a stage whisper.

But Vix was trying to get in on the Aidan-killing. She couldn't get her hands on the hammer so she leapt on his back and grabbed on to his face, digging her nails into his cheeks as hard as she could. Aidan swung his good arm round and caught her flush in the temple, and Vicky went sprawling across the room. It was a good hard hit – she was seeing stars now, so she went out to where Paul was waiting and the whole family pegged it down the road in case Aidan got the better of Sean and came looking.

Inside the house Aidan was taking a battering. However hard he was, he only had one good arm, and Sean's Forces experience meant he could channel the adrenalin. He was giving Aidan a lot of punches in the ribs and stomach, and there had been the odd crack of a rib and Aidan's innards were starting to throb to tell him they really weren't happy with this situation. The two of them were butting heads like there was no tomorrow. Just when he was thinking he might pass out, Aidan managed to bring his knee up between Sean's legs and give him five or six straight in the knackers. After the third or fourth Sean's grip on Aidan lessened and Aidan took the chance to reach out and grab the scissors that were lying off to the side. He brought the scissors up just as Sean got him by the throat and started to squeeze. They went into Sean's side under the armpit, about halfway in, and Sean's whole body stiffened. So Aidan pulled the scissors out and rammed them back in again as hard as he could, right up to the handles this time, the big loop that your fingers go through and the little loop that your thumb goes through. Sean stopped squeezing. It was like his attention had turned off Aidan and inward towards his own body. Aidan was able to push him away and get up into a crouching position.

His whole body was prickling with different pains from his elbow to his belly and ribs and his cheeks where Vicky had gouged him with her nails. He was dizzy so he stayed where he was for a moment, watching Sean make a face of agony and paw at the scissors which were a bit too far round for him to get a good grip on. It looked like they had gone in a bit above his heart but it was hard to tell. Sean was struggling to breathe but Aidan was panting heavily, and the sound seemed louder and louder in the quiet house. Bartholomew was still lying down between the easy chair and the gas fire. Then Aidan heard a siren and struggled to his feet, left the house and set off in a jog down the road.

What came out afterwards was a picture of Samuel L. Jackson or someone, on the rampage, staying one step ahead of the police and dealing with his enemies one by one. That was how people talked about it on social media, anyway. It was like, Aidan was taking revenge, so that made all the violence OK. The way he managed to move across Sheffield setting fire to portakabins under the nose of the police helicopter made him into a hero. It was the fact he had made a fool of the police that people really warmed to. Of course, loads of middle-class know-alls piled in saying he was just a thug and what was there to admire, and when you put it like that it was hard to argue. But if you were up in court for criminal damage and had no qualifications or prospects, or you had had your benefits stopped because hadn't been able to afford the bus fare to the job centre, or you owed eight grand on a five hundred quid loan, or were trapped in a loveless relationship and had chronic depression and acne, to see someone stand up and say, 'I don't give a fuck,' was something beautiful.

Then a load more people who didn't get it piled in with comments like, 'I got nothing either I dont go on a killin spree,' 'Get a job like the rest of us,' and 'These people arnt gonna stop gonna be islamic Law here unless we do something mark my words.'

And of course the day after it got on the national news, there was a column in the *Guardian* headlined, 'Where did it all go wrong? Why Aidan Wilson is the folk hero Britain deserves.' And then exclusives in the *Mirror* and the *Express* with some of the people Aidan had hurt, saying how he had ruined their lives, as well as a piece on Jasmine in the *Sun* that was half 'Grieving mum asks what happened to her boy' and half 'She produced a monster.'

All in all everyone got into a kind of frenzy imagining Aidan speeding across town like in *The French Connection*, setting off fire hydrants and leaning over the back of the car seat to let off one, two, three rounds from a stub-nosed Beretta at the chasing cops.

The reality was that once he got a hundred yards down the road from Vicky's house he ducked up a side street and hurried on as fast as he could, down a ginnel treading in dogshits and through to another part of the estate, all the time doing a sort of lolloping jog that was about as fast as an six-year-old on a tricycle, because of his broken elbow and the injuries to his ribs and belly. The police could have picked him up in about five minutes, but it was midnight on a Saturday so they were stretched to breaking point dealing with the drunks in the city centre. There had also been the fire at the car wash and that had tied up a couple of cars all evening. They didn't connect it yet with this call-out up in Foxhill, which as far as they knew was just another domestic.

It was only when they arrived at Vicky Shaw's house and found Sean with a pair of scissors sticking out of his oxter and Bartholomew blood-soaked and hardly breathing next to him, that they started to take it seriously. Once they had got hold of Vicky, Paul and the kids and heard Aidan's name, the computer flashed up that this was the same guy that South Wales Police wanted to talk to about the murder in Swansea, and that was the moment they diverted the helicopter from tracking joyriders in Wybourn and made Aidan Wilson their top priority for the night.

By this time Aidan had made it up to Grenoside where Amy and Martin were living now, in one of the new estates where the walls were thin as Rizlas but the front doors had fake marble pillars on either side, and the whole place had the feel of a well-tended graveyard.

The lights were on at Amy and Martin's house. Martin came to the door. 'Hey up,' he said, and stood aside to let Aidan in.

'Hey up,' said Aidan. They both used a serious tone that meant they knew about what had happened to Jay, but they didn't mention him, and Martin didn't mention the state Aidan was in.

Amy did though. She was stood in the middle of the living room trying to work the ipod.

'Fucking hell,' she said. 'You look rough, bruv. Rough as

fucking worse than I feel. Come and have a listen to The Cure. That bastard won't let me have another drink.'

She tried to have a dance with Aidan, so he smiled at her and then took Martin off into the kitchen for a word.

'Dunt she know?' he asked.

Martin said, 'I said to Jasmine, I'm not telling her while she's pissed. In the morning.' What he didn't say was that he had just had a second call, from Kayla, who had driven down from Barnsley and arrived at the hospital in time to be told that Jay had died in surgery. He reckoned that Aidan didn't need to know that any more than Amy.

Aidan asked if he could borrow a car. 'A shit one,' he said. 'Summat run-of-the-mill like a Focus.'

Martin said all his cars were at the saleroom, but there was his Qashqai out the front.

Aidan said, 'Aye, whatever.'

Martin asked what it was for. Aidan said it was better he didn't know. So Martin picked up the keys off the kitchen table and gave them to him.

Aidan said, 'I'm going away for a bit. Say I nicked it. And keep your mouth shut.'

'I will,' said Martin. 'You stupid bugger. Good luck.'

57

I T WAS JUST starting to get light, getting on for five o'clock in the morning, when Jennyviv's husband Mal got up to go for a piss and saw this black SUV sitting by the gates. He often couldn't sleep, thinking about local government contracts, and after his piss he would stand and look out of the window at the wet driveway and the trees in the avenue, trying not to wake up any further but knowing if he went back to bed straight away his mind would only keep racing. Sometimes, though he didn't tell Jennyviv this, he tossed himself off in the bathroom and that helped him get to sleep again. But today, there was this SUV on the road outside the gates, with its engine idling. He could see the fumes from its exhaust frothing up behind. He stood and watched it for a minute, thinking. And then he went in to the bedroom and woke Jennyviv.

'What is it?' she said, coming round.

He said, 'It might be burglars. I was going to ring the police, but then I thought it might be one of your lot. A lost puppy.'

She came and looked out of the window with him, and then said that it might be, but he should ring the police anyway.

While he was doing that she pulled on her dressing gown and slippers and went out to the car.

Aidan wound down the window. 'Hey up,' he said.

'Aidan, what are you doing here?'

He broke eye contact and looked ahead out of the windscreen as if the road in front ran a long, long way.

'What are you doing here?' she said again, and put her hand on the car door. He looked down at it. She said, 'You know you can't come here. I thought I'd made that clear. Mal's ringing the police.'

'Is he?' said Aidan.

'I told him to. Aidan, look at the state of you. What's happened?'

Aidan thought about it for a few seconds and then said, 'I'd better go,' but he didn't.

Jennyviv said, in a louder voice as if she was trying to get through to him, 'What's happened?'

But he wouldn't say. He put the car in gear, looked down at her hand till she took it off the car door, said, 'Bye,' and pulled away.

Mal came out, still on the line to the emergency services, cross that she had come out on her own. 'Who was it?' he said. 'What did he want?'

Jennyviv said, 'I don't know.' She told him to tell the police it was a man called Aidan Wilson, and after a pause the operator said they were sending someone straight round. 'That doesn't sound good,' said Mal.

They made coffee while they waited. That was the year Mal went private on his sinuses and took his hours down to four days a week, and after that he slept a lot better.

By this time it was a double murder enquiry. The police had established that Aidan Wilson, the man they were looking for in relation to the death of Daniel John Crease in Swansea, was the same man who had absconded from the scene in Foxhill.

Sean Shaw, the man who had been stabbed with kitchen scissors, was stable in hospital, but Michael Bartholomew had died in the ambulance, apparently as a result of a single blow to the head.

Vicky had said to the family liaison officer that they were lucky Aidan hadn't pulled the trigger and shot them all. There was a moment of horror and alarm and scepticism all rolled into one.

'Are you saying that Mr Wilson had a gun?' said the liaison officer, and Vicky said, 'Yes,' without missing a beat.

'What kind of gun?' said the liaison officer, like she totally wasn't convinced.

Vicky said, 'A revolver, like, a hand gun, or summat. He was waving it around, saying he was going to kill us and all the coppers too.'

Then the liaison officer turned to Vicky's fella Paul and asked if he had seen the gun. And he hesitated, and then said, 'Yes.'

The serious incident team discussed it, and decided that although there were doubts about whether the suspect was armed, they couldn't take any chances. Local journalists were asking questions and ringing up their contacts in Swansea, and everything was moving rather quickly. So, in the interests of public safety, they arranged a hasty media conference where they said that they were looking for a man suspected of two murders and several other serious crimes. This man may be armed and dangerous, and must not under any circumstances be approached by a member of the public. And for the next eighteen hours Aidan was all over Facebook, Twitter and BBC Look North.

58

AFTER HE LEFT Jennyviv, Aidan drove up through Oughtibridge and Deepcar and over the Woodhead Pass towards Greater Manchester. The helicopter was still out and the cameras at the lights would have picked up his reg number if the police had known it, so he figured Jennyviv and her husband hadn't thought to get it. Lucky the Qashqai was an automatic – his left arm was useless, and throbbing like a bastard. Compared to that, the pain in his chest and head was nothing. But it was hard to breathe. He could only go in steady shallow breaths, or a fire lit up in his lungs worse than any pain he'd ever known.

He drove along with the black reservoir on his left hand side with his phone going off. It was Jasmine. The first few times he ignored it, but it kept going off so he answered.

'Mam,' he said.

He heard Jasmine say, 'Aidan,' but then there was a pause before another voice started speaking.

It said, 'Is that you Aidan? Things have . . .'

He hung up, wound down the car window and chucked the phone out.

By the time he was heading up by Oldham and Rochdale, he was starting to get seriously hungry. He hadn't eaten since he was on the coach. So he pulled into a garage and bought a chicken tikka pasty and a tube of Pringles, and a big bottle of Lucozade to wash it down with. There was an industrial estate round the corner. Since it was Sunday morning and the place was deserted, he drove to the far end and pulled up outside a builder's merchants, ate the food and got in the back seat to get his head down for a bit.

He couldn't get to sleep, with the pain and the excitement of it all, but he rested his eyes for an hour and that made him feel better. He moved back into the front seat to drive off but closed his eyes again for a moment, and he must have fallen asleep because the next thing was he was being woken up by someone tapping on the window.

There was a woman there saying, 'You looking for business, love?'

He wound down the window and they looked each other over.

'It's the dregs on a Sunday morning,' she said.

'You're telling me,' said Aidan.

She said, 'Are you bothered then, or not?' and he was about to tell her to sling her hook when he saw a security guard peering over at them from his van.

'Why not,' said Aidan, and she walked round and got in the passenger side.

The security guard was walking over. Aidan started the engine and pulled away. The man watched them go, and Aidan could see him in the rear view mirror, standing on the road looking after them.

A mile or so down the road he pulled up and told the tom to get out. She cut up rough, calling him a poof and a fucking time waster, so he rummaged in the glove compartment and gave her Martin's TomTom.

'What the fuck am I supposed to do with that?' she said, and she had a point.

He found himself on the Bury road, but the pain in his chest was getting worse. He had to breathe in really carefully or it was like he was being stabbed, so bad that once he passed out for a second and veered into the other lane, and only the other car sounding its horn saved his life. And his head was throbbing worse than ever too. Even though he had had the sleep, it was an effort to think straight and remember what he was doing.

He decided to find a Boots or something, where he could get some tablets. The next grim line of shops he came to, he slowed down, and there was a local pharmacy, open on a Sunday for the junkies. He pulled up and sat in the car for a while gathering his thoughts, and then went in.

There were a couple of biddies waiting for their prescriptions, one sitting on a plastic chair and the other browsing the wrist supports.

'I've come for me methadone,' said Aidan to the blonde assistant.

She smiled insincerely. 'Can I have your prescription please?'

'Lost it,' he said.

She said, 'Are you registered with us?'

Aidan looked her for a minute and then leaned over the counter and said, 'I need some methadone.'

She called over her shoulder, 'Frank,' and at that moment the pharmacist was coming anyway with the biddies' goodie bags. He handed them over, saying, 'Mrs Jarvis, Mrs Patel.' All the while, he and his assistant and Mrs Jarvis and Mrs Patel were watching Aidan to see what he would do, but he just stood there waiting till the two old biddies left the shop.

They hung around outside trying to peer through the window.

Frank the pharmacist started saying, 'I'm afraid if you don't have your prescription . . .' but Aidan reached across, grabbed him by the lapel of his white coat and pulled him forwards over the counter. Their heads connected and Frank's glasses boinged off his face towards the Hall's Soothers. Then Frank was sprawled on the lavender carpet tiles, not sparko but not exactly with it either, and Aidan turned to face the blonde assistant just as her finger pressed the alarm button under the counter.

'You shunta fuckin done that,' he said, and you could tell by the expression on her face that she was thinking the exact same thing.

Then he stood over the pharmacist acting like he was going to brain him while she got him a shot of the green stuff. He necked it, but the pharmacist looking up at him from the floor saw how he was grimacing and holding himself so carefully, and said, 'Methadone'll take a while to take effect. If you need pain relief, there are more effective options.'

Aidan was looking nervously out the window in case the old biddies were still around and maybe calling for help. The pain in his chest was really bad. The pharmacist was saying about various drugs and asking exactly what kind of pain it was and where, and how did he get the injuries because that might make a difference too. So Aidan told him he had a broken arm and had taken a kicking, and then waited while the blonde assistant got the right drugs under the pharmacist's instructions. It took a while because she was shaking so much and at first she got the wrong drugs, and then there was a stand-off while Aidan said, 'What if you're fucking me over, giving me a sleeping pill or something,' and the pharmacist said, 'No, we wouldn't do that,' and so on. In the end Aidan figured he had nothing to lose so he took what they gave him. The assistant opened a bottle of Buxton water for him to wash them down. He said, 'Thanks.'

Frank the pharmacist said, 'It's OK you know, you don't have to keep running,' and 'We can help you,' but Aidan ignored him and looked out of the window. There were no blue flashing lights out there but something was definitely up. There was no one walking past the window and no cars either, and that seemed odd, even on a Sunday morning.

The truth was that earlier in the morning the police had turned up at Martin and Amy's looking for Aidan, and so of course Martin had had to tell them Aidan had nicked the car or he would go down for accessory. Then the security guard up at the industrial estate had called in the Qashqai's reg number for kerb-crawling, some zealous sod at police control had put the number into the national database, and bingo. So as soon as Aidan had come through the automatic cameras at the last big roundabout, an armed response unit had been despatched.

Since Aidan was staying put, Frank the pharmacist started saying things like, 'You've got what you wanted, now go,' but Aidan told him to shut up. Then Frank seemed to get a bit drowsy and the assistant said, 'He's diabetic, he needs his insulin,' but Aidan didn't know if it was a trick.

Frank said, 'At least let Megan go,' and Aidan looked at the assistant's face with its frightened eyes and wanted to let her go but couldn't think.

So then Frank said, 'Just go, the longer you wait the more likely the police'll turn up.'

Aidan thought a bit more and then went over to the shelf

and took a BaByliss hairdryer out of its box. Then he said to Megan, 'Come with me,' and went to the front of the shop keeping her in front of him. He couldn't see much through the glass of the door, so he just opened it, pushed her out and followed her.

They got a couple of steps and Aidan could see there were coppers with guns covering the shop from both directions. He had Megan in front of him and held the hairdryer up to her head with his good hand. With the knackered hand he tried to keep a hold of the back of her white coat, but he could hardly get a grip and straight away she pulled away and ran across into the empty road towards PaddyPower.

Maybe there was a shouted warning, maybe not, but as soon as she was clear the police opened fire. Three shots struck him in the chest and the fourth went through his hand and then into his abdomen, which is what the pathologist called his belly. Aidan stepped back against the shattering window of the shop and then toppled over sideways like a sack of spuds. There was blood coming out of the holes straight away and the armed police were running up covering him with their weapons, and the scene was secured. Aidan was taken to A&E at Fairfield but pronounced dead on arrival.

Megan had a few puffs on her inhaler and a tea with three sugars from Starbucks, but it took twelve months of seeing a counsellor to regain her confidence in dealing with the public.

Frank was taken in a separate ambulance and had to stay in overnight in case of concussion. He said to Megan later the diabetic thing had been a good idea, but it was best to be completely honest in a situation like that and next time just say that he had had a blow to the head and needed medical attention.

Megan said, 'Next time?'

He gave her a hug and though he smelt of old-fashioned soap and it felt weird being touched by your boss, the two of them were kind to each other after that and got on pretty well, until Megan got a better offer from a hospital dispensary in Cheshire.

When the chief constable heard, he said, 'Bloody great that is, another IPCC job,' and sliced his tee shot.

59

A IDAN WAS THE top story on the ITV evening bul-
letin, and the third story on BBC. Social media blew up
in a shitstorm of opinions, with half the world calling him a
hero and half worse than Hitler. The Britain First lot called
him a terrorist, and middle-class lefties called him a symptom
of a wider problem in society, and then came the sick jokes
and an animated GIF that went viral.

Others were more interested in scanning Facebook for
'Porcupine Tastes His First Pumpkin, And Can't Contain
His Excitement' and 'Ten celebrities who used to be HOT'
and 'She orders fries and a coke. You won't BELIEVE what
happens next.' And then Miley Cyrus slipped a boob at some
awards do and Aidan was off the newsfeeds forever.

Back on the estate he was news for a while yet. Irene at the
taxi office said, 'That's another young lad they've let down.
He never had a chance.' Gemma cried a bit and said that
could be her little brother in a few years time, and she let
Brendan hold her hand and whisper, 'It's a tragedy,' and so
on. When Brendan left the office for his Beighton pick-up he
had a massive smile on his face.

Ian the ex-bouncer said a twat like that had it coming, and
when they heard that, Carl and Connor steamed up to the
social club and told him if only he wasn't such an old cunt
they would break his fucking legs.

Billy told Steve about Aidan killing Creasey, and then

about him being dead himself, and Steve broke down again, sobbing in his wheelchair like there was nothing good left in the world, saying, 'He did it for our Suze, Billy,' but Billy sat on the arm of the sofa and made a wry face.

Jasmine had two funerals to arrange, but because of the circumstances they were both delayed. So she sat in Kayla's living room smoking fag after fag, and first Jay's body and then Aidan's were released. After the funerals she said goodbye to Kayla and Stephen, who had been going straight for nearly six months, and went back to Sheffy.

They had kept her shifts for her at the Cutlers Arms and she spent most of her time in there, pulling pints with a face like death and snarling at anyone who spoke to her. And if anyone came in for the first time and said to their mate, 'What's up with that grim cow,', their mate would sit them down and tell them the story of what had happened to the barmaid's sons, how all three had died and left her bitter as hell.

And when the story finished they would say to their mate, 'Jesus Christ.' And there would be a little gap and then they would say, 'Same again?'

Acknowledgements

This book would not have been possible without the medieval sagas of Icelanders, and deep gratitude is offered to their authors and English translators. *Nutcase* is an adaptation of *The Saga of Grettir the Strong*, and particular thanks are due to its anonymous author and to the translations by Denton Fox and Hermann Pálsson, and by Bernard Scudder.